SEEING IN THE DARK:
MARGARET ATWOOD'S *CAT'S EYE*

Canadian Fiction Studies

Additional volumes are available.

Seeing in the Dark:
MARGARET ATWOOD'S

Cat's Eye

Arnold E. Davidson

ECW PRESS

THE CANADA COUNCIL | LE CONSEIL DES ARTS
FOR THE ARTS | DU CANADA
SINCE 1957 | DEPUIS 1957

We acknowledge the support of the Canada
Council for the Arts in our publishing program.

This book has been published with the assistance
of grants from the Ontario Arts Council.

CANADIAN CATALOGUING IN PUBLICATION DATA

Davidson, Arnold E., 1936–
Seeing in the dark : Margaret Atwood's Cat's eye

(Canadian fiction studies ; 35)
Includes bibliographical references and index.
ISBN 1-55022-312-7

I. Atwood, Margaret, 1939– . Cat's eye.
I. Title. II. Series.

PS8501.T86C33 1997   C813'.54   C97-930388-5
PR9199.3.A88C333 1997

The cover features a reproduction of the
dust-wrapper from the first edition of
Cat's Eye, courtesy of The Thomas Fisher
Rare Books Library, University of Toronto.
Frontispiece photograph courtesy Canapress Archives.

Design and imaging by ECW Type & Art, Oakville, Ontario.
Printed by AGMV l'Imprimeur, Cap-Saint-Ignace, Quebec.

Distributed by General Distribution Services,
30 Lesmill Road, Don Mills, Ontario M3B 2T6.

Published by ECW PRESS,
2120 Queen Street East,
Toronto, Ontario M4E 1E2.

http://www.ecw.ca/press

PRINTED AND BOUND IN CANADA

Table of Contents

A Note on the Author

Arnold E. Davidson was born in Cardston, Alberta, and grew up on a small ranch just outside of Waterton Lakes National Park. He attended the University of Chicago from which he received a BA in Anthropology and an MA in English. He received his PhD, also in English, from the State University of New York at Binghamton, where he wrote a dissertation on Joseph Conrad directed by Robert Kroetsch. That process directed him back to Canadian literature, and he soon began publishing primarily on contemporary Canadian writers, particularly Robert Kroetsch and Margaret Atwood. He is one of the founding co-presidents of the Margaret Atwood Society and has coedited *The Art of Margaret Atwood*, a collection of essays on her poetry and fiction. He has edited *Studies on Canadian Literature: Introductory and Critical Essays* for the Modern Language Association and has published books on Joseph Conrad, Jean Rhys, Mordecai Richler, and Joy Kogawa. His most recent book, *Coyote Country: Fictions of the Canadian West* (published by Duke University Press in 1994), won the Association of Canadian Studies in the United States Publication Award. He is also the author of some eighty academic articles, most of them on Canadian literature. After teaching, first, at Elmhurst College in Elmhurst, Illinois, and then in the English Department and the Canadian Studies Program at Michigan State University, he is now a Research Professor of Canadian Studies at Duke University.

REFERENCES AND ACKNOWLEDGEMENTS

All page references to *Cat's Eye* are given parenthetically in the text and are to the original hardcover edition published in Toronto by McClelland and Stewart in 1988.

I would like to thank the Rockefeller Foundation for awarding me a Bellagio Research Fellowship which allowed me to begin working out my reading of the novel. I am grateful, too, to Duke University and the Canadian Studies Center at Duke for unstinting financial and intellectual support, and I would particularly like to thank two colleagues, Professors George Elliott Clarke and Sylvia Ross, for their careful and constructive reading of the manuscript. I am also indebted to two of my research assistants, Heather Rogers and Madeleine Vala, for their work on this project and doubly so to Heather Rogers in that she also served as an exemplary typist. I would here also thank Robert Lecker for his patience and support.

Finally, I would like to dedicate the book to Charles and Susan and to Judy and to thank the three of them for providing the two tables on which much of the final draft was completed.

Seeing in the Dark:
Margaret Atwood's
Cat's Eye

Chronology

1939   Margaret Eleanor Atwood, the second of three children, is born November 18 in Ottawa to Margaret Dorothy (née Killam) Atwood and Carl Edmund Atwood. Her brother, Harold, is born in 1937, and her sister, Ruth, in 1951.

1939–45   The family spends winters in Ottawa but lives the rest of the year in northern Ontario and Quebec where her father works as a forest entomologist.

1945   Family moves to Sault Ste. Marie.

1951   Family moves to Toronto, where her father accepts a teaching position at the University of Toronto, but continues to live much of each year in the north woods, where her father conducts his research when he isn't teaching.

1952–57   Attends Leaside High School in Toronto and writes prose and verse for the school literary magazine.

1957–61   Attends Victoria College of the University of Toronto and graduates with an Honours BA in English. Publishes prose and poems in college magazines and also publishes poems in national journals such as *Canadian Forum* and *Tamarack Review*.

1961   Publishes a first book of poetry, *Double Persephone*, which wins the E.J. Pratt Medal.

1961–62   Attends Radcliffe College in Cambridge, MA, on a Woodrow Wilson Fellowship and receives an MA in English.

1963   Works as a market researcher in Toronto and completes her first novel, *Up in the Air So Blue*, which remains unpublished.

1964–65   Teaches English at the University of British Columbia in Vancouver.

1965–67   Begins a PhD in English at Harvard University in Cambridge, MA, but does not complete the degree.

1966   Publishes *The Circle Game* (poetry), which wins the Governor General's Award.

1967   Marries James Polk and moves to Montreal, Quebec, where she teaches English at Sir George Williams College (now part of Concordia University).

1968   Publishes *The Animals in That Country* (poetry), which wins the Centennial Commission Poetry Competition.

1969   Publishes *The Edible Woman* (novel). Wins Union Poetry Prize awarded by *Poetry* (Chicago).

1969–70   Teaches creative writing at the University of Alberta in Edmonton.

1970   Publishes *The Journals of Susanna Moodie* (poetry) and *Procedures for Underground* (poetry).

1971   Publishes *Power Politics* (poetry). Joins editorial board of House of Anansi Press.

1971–72   Teaches Canadian literature at York University, Toronto.

1972   Publishes *Surfacing* (novel) and *Survival: A Thematic Guide to Canadian Literature* (literary criticism).

1972–73   Serves as writer-in-residence at the University of Toronto.

1973   Divorces James Polk and moves to Alliston, Ontario, with novelist Graeme Gibson. Receives honorary degree from Trent University (many more are subsequently awarded by other universities). Joins the board of directors of the Canadian Civil Liberties Union.

1974   Publishes *You Are Happy* (poetry).

1976   Publishes *Lady Oracle* (novel) and *Selected Poems*. She and Graeme Gibson have a daughter, Eleanor Jess Atwood Gibson.

1977   Publishes *Dancing Girls* (short stories), which wins the City of Toronto Book Award, the Canadian Booksellers' Association Award, and the Periodical Distributors of Canada Short Fiction Award. Also publishes *Days of the Rebels: 1815–1840* (history).

1978   Publishes *Two-Headed Poems* (poetry) and *Up in the Tree* (children's literature).

1979   Publishes *Life Before Man* (novel).

1980   Publishes, with Joyce Barkhouse, *Anna's Pet* (children's literature). Elected vice-president of the Writers' Union of Canada and moves, with her family, to Toronto.

1981   Publishes *True Stories* (poetry) and *Bodily Harm* (novel). Receives Molson Award and Guggenheim Fellowship and is named Companion of the Order of Canada. Elected president of the Writers' Union of Canada for a one-year term.

1982   Publishes *Second Words: Selected Critical Prose* and edits *The New Oxford Book of Canadian Verse in English*. Awarded the Welsh Arts Council International Writer's Prize.

1983   Publishes *Murder in the Dark: Short Fictions and Prose Poems* and *Bluebeard's Egg* (short stories), which wins the Periodical Distributors of Canada Short Fiction Award and the Foundation for the Advancement of Canadian Letters Book of the Year Award.

1984   Publishes *Interlunar* (poetry). Elected president of P.E.N. International, Canadian Centre (English Speaking), for a two-year term.

1985   Publishes *The Handmaid's Tale* (novel), which wins the Governor General's Award, the Arthur C. Clarke Award for Best Science Fiction, the *Los Angeles Times* Fiction Award, and the Commonwealth Literary Regional Prize. Serves as MFA Honorary (Visiting) Chair in creative writing at the University of Alabama in Tuscaloosa, AL.

1986   Publishes *Selected Poems II* and coedits, with Robert Weaver, *The Oxford Book of Canadian Short Stories in English*. Appointed Berg (Visiting) Chair at New York University in New York, NY, and is named Woman of the Year by *Ms.* magazine.

1987   Publishes *The Canlit Foodbook*. Elected Fellow of the Royal Society of Canada and is named Humanist of the Year by the American Humanist Society. Serves as writer-in-residence at Macquarie University in Sydney, Australia.

1988   Publishes *Cat's Eye* (novel), which wins the City of Toronto Book Award, the Coles Book of the Year Award, the Canadian Booksellers' Association Award, and the Foundation for the Advancement of Canadian Letters Book of the Year Award. Elected Foreign Honorary Member in Literature by the American Academy of Arts and Sciences and receives YWCA Woman of Distinction Award.

1989   Coedits, with Shannon Ravenel, *The Best American Short Stories 1989*. Serves as writer-in-residence at Trinity University in San Antonio, TX.

1990   Publishes *For the Birds* (children's literature). Becomes member of the Order of Ontario and receives Harvard Centennial Medal.

1991   Publishes *Wilderness Tips* (short stories), which wins the Trillium Book Award and the Periodical Marketers of Canada Book of the Year Award.

1992   Publishes *Good Bones* (short fictions and prose poems).

1993   Publishes *The Robber Bride* (novel), which wins the Trillium Book Award, the Commonwealth Writers' Canadian and Caribbean Region Prize, and the Canadian Authors' Association Novel of the Year Award. Also publishes *Good Bones and Simple Murders* (a combination of *Good Bones* and *Murder in the Dark* with one new piece added) and coedits, with Barry Callaghan, *The Poetry of Gwendolyn MacEwen, Volume One: The Early Years*.

1994   Named Chevalier dans l'Ordre des Arts et des Lettres by the French Government. Coedits, with Barry Callaghan, *The Poetry of Gwendolyn MacEwen, Volume Two: The Later Years*.

1995   Publishes *Morning in the Burned House* (poetry), *Strange Things: The Malevolent North in Canadian Literature* (literary criticism), and *Princess Prunella and the Purple Peanut* (children's literature). Coedits, with Robert Weaver, *The New Oxford Book of Canadian Short Stories in English*.

1996   Publishes *Alias Grace* (novel).

The Importance of the Work

The six novels that Margaret Atwood published before *Cat's Eye*, not to mention her numerous other books of short stories and poetry, had already established her as a major contemporary writer, and *The Handmaid's Tale*, the immediately preceding novel, had especially done so. Far more people, particularly outside of Canada, were reading her fiction and more critics were praising her work. To be both commercially successful and critically acclaimed is a dual accomplishment achieved by few authors. By the time *Cat's Eye* appeared, any new Atwood novel would be important simply because there was now another work in which to appreciate her dry wit and sharp intelligence, another book in which to weigh her ongoing critique of contemporary Canada and the world, and in which to see her give new twists to her basic feminist concerns — surfacing, power politics, circle games, bodily harm (to borrow from just a few earlier titles).

But *Cat's Eye*, like all of Atwood's novels, is not just another Atwood novel. One of her strengths as a writer is the way she reworks material from her earlier books but does not simply rewrite them. Central concerns inform all her fictions; fictional formulas do not. *Cat's Eye*, for example, partly evokes all of Atwood's previous novels — *The Edible Woman*'s critique of consumerism and the commodification of women, *Surfacing*'s interrogation of female identity, *Lady Oracle*'s protagonist both victimized as a girl by other little girls and transmuting childhood suffering into art, the vast deployment of time implicit in *Life Before Man*, *Bodily Harm*'s poetics of pain, the therapeutic telling of a painful personal story in *The Handmaid's Tale*. But it evokes them with a difference, and Elaine Risley, the protagonist of *Cat's Eye*, does not particularly resemble any of Atwood's earlier female protagonists, even though her story closely parallels the unnamed narrator's account, in *Surfacing*, of her early family life in the woods during World War II and her subsequent affair with her art teacher, as well as Joan's telling, in *Lady Oracle*, of her childhood traumas in Toronto's ravines. My own sense is that these similarities are roughly analogous to the connections between Charles Dickens's *David Copperfield* and *Great Expectations*. All writers have their subjects, but sometimes an older writer pointedly returns to a topic treated earlier to do it fuller justice, to portray it with a more developed art and vision. So Dickens in *Great Expectations* rewrites the story of the orphan boy with larger implications and deeper resonances than he achieved in *Oliver Twist* or *David Copperfield*, and Atwood in *Cat's Eye* similarly writes of young girls at play and war in a time of war far more persuasively than she did in *Surfacing* and *Lady Oracle*.

Cat's Eye is in some ways the most personal of Atwood's novels. Clearly, she has borrowed substantially from her own life in giving Elaine that girlhood split between Toronto and the north woods, and in giving her, too, a successful career as a woman artist. Atwood, we know, has long been interested in the visual arts, and at one point in her childhood she "wanted to be a painter" (Ingersoll, *Conversations* 60). She has done the illustrations for a number of her book covers — *Power Politics*, *True Stories*, and *Interlunar*, for example — and has also published cartoons and comic strips such as *Kanadian Kultchur Komix* (featuring "Survivalwoman") which appeared in *This Magazine*. But much of *Cat's Eye* is self-evidently not autobiographical. Atwood is an author, not a painter. She does not live in Vancouver. She does not have two daughters and is not married to the owner of a travel agency. Her brother was not killed in a plane hijacking. The book is a novel, not a fictionalized autobiography. It is, however, a novel that might be termed "meta-autobiographical" in that it is about narrating an account of a life, and that accounting also involves the author.[1] Atwood, pushing fifty, portrays a painter of approximately the same age who relates the tribulations of her early life and subsequent successful career. The novel, as a portrait of the artist as a no-longer-young woman, partly superimposes the figure of the author onto the figure of the protagonist, and does so most obviously with respect to key questions: What are the pluses and the minuses of success and aging for a woman (a summing up also central to Atwood's "Aging Female Poet . . ." poems in her

Selected Poems 11)? How does one's childhood continue to shape one's adult life? How do we come to terms with who we are and with the world in which we live?

These are questions that we all face in some form, and that, too, is part of the power and effect of *Cat's Eye*. More particularly, we all carry a legacy of childhood pain — memories of both injuries done to us and of injuries we inflicted on others. On a personal note, I cannot read *Cat's Eye* without vividly recalling one of the most shameful episodes from my own childhood. In a small, poor community, and attending a four-room rural school, we early picked out one grade-one girl as the disgusting embodiment of all we didn't want to be, and teased, tormented, and ostracized her all through grade school. I was particularly assiduous in doing so because I deeply suspected that if it wasn't her it would be me. As Atwood well knows, we can all too easily inflict harm on others, and children do not have to be left alone on a tropical island, as in William Golding's *Lord of the Flies*, to do what even little girls can do perfectly "naturally."

That "naturally" is in quotation marks because the human "natural" is always substantially socially constructed. From her first novel, *The Edible Woman*, to her most recent, *Alias Grace*, Atwood has again and again assessed the mechanics of the social construction of the female individual in a patriarchal society. The doubleness and dividedness that her female protagonists experience — the hints of a missing twin, the suggestions of a second identity, the doppelgängers and secret sharers they so regularly encounter — attest to their sense of not belonging in the world in which they find themselves and their feeling that some crucial aspects of the self have been lost or repressed. How devastatingly extensive this loss can be and how programmatically it can be inflicted is powerfully portrayed in *The Handmaid's Tale*, with its account of how Gilead forces women into rigorously defined roles and even state-sanctioned prostitution (the Handmaids as well as the Jezebels) that is also rape in that the consequence for women who refuse to have sex with various members of the ruling male elite is death. We don't, however, live in Gilead, and, despite Atwood's careful grounding of the details of Gilead in the real world, the book is a dystopia. Furthermore, suffering and loss can take place without being officially sanctioned or imposed by society. *Cat's Eye* charts such suffering in a fully rendered present and immediate past — particularly the forties, fifties, and sixties — not in a projected future. A seventies slogan asserted that "the personal is the political." In *Cat's Eye*, however, Atwood conversely reads the political back into the personal. We see how Cordelia can pass her father's disapproval of his daughter onto Elaine and how Elaine can later pass it back; we see, too, how deep the shared pain of both of them goes and how it is partly transcended, becoming for Elaine an impetus to art, but how it also remains a permanent burden, with the middle-aged Elaine still haunted by her childhood, and Cordelia pushed to mental collapse and perhaps even suicide.

Power, however privately it is applied, always has a social context and dimension. *Cat's Eye* foregrounds three such contexts — patriarchy, war (particularly World War ii), and imperialism (with its attendant racism). Patriarchy is the most basic and obvious of these groundings. As a child, Elaine notes that Cordelia's father conveys the sense that his judgement of you is absolute and correct whereas yours of him, if you dared hazard one, would be wrong and irrelevant. The privilege of patriarchy, moreover, works on both a familial and social level, and on both levels women are seen as not measuring up to the standards that men set. Consumer society, we see again and again in the novel, sells female anxiety, the sense of female "imperfections," and both men and capitalism profit from the selling. Patriarchal-like claims of the rightness of one group and the wrongness of another also underlie both war and empire. The parallel between war and sexism is particularly suggested in the novel by the way the children play at war, for with Stephen's early directives — "lie down, you're dead" — his little sister Elaine is learning to be both female and victim. Imperialism similarly entails modes of deeming others inferior and "natural" victims. Miss Lumley, the worst teacher Elaine encounters in primary school, is a proponent of and apologist for the British Empire and advocates ideas of British superiority, ideas Elaine early questions: "Wolfe's name sounds like something you'd call a dog, but he conquered the French. This is puzzling, because I've seen French people, there are lots of them up north, so he couldn't have conquered all of them" (80). Also significant in this context are the three muses of one of Elaine's later paintings, Mr. Banerji, Mrs. Finestein, and Miss Stuart, all of whom, as adults, endured pain analogous to that which Elaine suffered as a child. Mr. Banerji, one of her father's students from India, was not

16

given a position he merited at the University of Toronto because he was the wrong race. Elaine baby-sat for Mrs. Finestein shortly after the war and later asks, "Who knows what death-camp ashes blew daily through [her] head." Miss Stuart, Elaine's favourite teacher, "was in exile, from plundered Scotland still declining, three thousand miles away" (407). Gender, war, race, and colonial rule are all conflated as different means of producing an "other" to whom one can do bad things without judging oneself bad for doing so. All of these issues are effectively explored in *Cat's Eye*, and part of the effect derives from the way Elaine is both victim and victimizer, for she knows both sides of the false divide, and from both sides looks at the dark reality of what humans can do to one another.

Novels, however, are works of art more than they are disquisitions on history or anthropology or philosophy or cosmology or whatever. Atwood has noted that if she had an explicit message to convey she would rent a billboard. But she hasn't rented a billboard, she has written a work of fiction. The importance of that work depends more on the success of its art than on the substance of its meaning, although this distinction is itself a false dichotomy since the style and meaning of any novel are inextricably interconnected and the meaning emerges through the artistry rather than simply being dressed up by it. For me, *Cat's Eye* is most important because it is Atwood's most artistically accomplished novel thus far. That art will be assessed in detail in my "Reading of the Text." What I will note here is how Atwood grounds the novel in three other great literary ventures at seeing in the dark and so signals her large artistic intentions by staging a "daughterly" rewriting of Proust, Shakespeare, and Dante.[2]

First and most obviously, as a "remembrance of times past," *Cat's Eye* clearly parallels Marcel Proust's great novel, *A la recherche du temps perdu*. This literary debt is specifically acknowledged when Elaine has her own Proustian moment of reaccessing much that she has forgotten or, more accurately, repressed. In a scene to be more fully assessed later, she finds her old cat's eye marble and sees in it her "life entire" (398), thus reenacting a visual version of Marcel's tasting the madeleine. By recovering her previously lost memories, Elaine also recovers much of the world in which those memories are grounded. One of the attractions of the novel for readers old enough to remember World War II and immediately after is to see how much they have forgotten — how, for example, in the forties, long before

Star Wars and Toys Я Us, small boys played at war with cut-out glued-together paper airplanes and homemade wooden swords, or how "ultra-sharp" (112) teenaged girls dressed in the early fifties. For the reader, and even more for the protagonist, the novel is a Proustian foray into the darkness of times past to revisit, in memory, an otherwise lost world. As Robert Towers observes, "A social historian of the next century could find no better source [than *Cat's Eye*] for what middle-class children in Toronto — or, for that matter, most of the northern and midwestern United States — wore, ate, sang, or played with during the 1940s and 1950s" (50).

The novel explores a different darkness as well, the darkness of the human heart, which is particularly evoked by pervasive references to two of Shakespeare's plays, *Macbeth* and *King Lear*. The staging of *Macbeth* in the novel casts Cordelia's and then Elaine's betrayal of one another under the guise of friendship as a version of Macbeth's murder of Duncan under the guise of host, defender, and loyal subject. *Macbeth* also introduces themes of reversal and revenge. The tormentor is tormented in the novel just as the murderer is eventually murdered in the play. Indeed, Cordelia's fiasco at the first playing of *Macbeth* in the novel provides Elaine with her best ammunition for attacking Cordelia, who, as props manager, substituted a new cabbage for a rotten one, a cabbage that, wrapped in a white towel and passing for the cut-off head of Macbeth, bounces across the stage instead of landing with a flesh-sounding thud when thrown triumphantly down. " 'Bumpity bumpity bump, plop' " (246), Elaine devastatingly teases Cordelia after the show, another indication of how deep disguises go (they are officially best friends) and of how "There's no art / To find the mind's [or heart's] construction in the face" (*Macbeth* 1.4.13–14). Despite the occasionally displayed hearts in her later paintings, Elaine's art, like Shakespeare's, prominently features disguises, doubles, displacements, distorted reflections, and other such devices that remind us of how hard it is to see to the heart of things when it comes to humans and what they can do.

More specifically, Atwood, like Shakespeare, also makes much of "nothing." For Macbeth, life becomes finally "a tale / Told by an idiot, full of sound and fury, / Signifying nothing" (5.5.29–31). That "nothing" signifies throughout *Cat's Eye*, but *King Lear's* "nothing," even more than *Macbeth's*, also echoes throughout the novel. As R.D. Lane argues in "Cordelia's 'Nothing': The Character of Cordelia and Margaret Atwood's *Cat's Eye*," the novel "constitutes a reworking of . . . *King Lear*" (87), and Cordelia's "most . . . important role in both [the play and the novel] is [to embody] nothingness" (81). The loving daughter whose spoken "nothing" launches her father on his final fall to "nothing" and its attendant lessons of what it means to be "a poor, bare, forked" and "unaccommodated man" (*King Lear* 3.4.111–12) becomes the friend who reduces Elaine to nothing and is, in turn, similarly reduced herself. In both the play and the novel that "nothing" is hard to plumb, to measure, to map. How do we peer into the darkness of the meaninglessness and nothingness of human life? How can we see ourselves as only poor, bare, forked, and finally unaccommodated animals inhabiting a world that is itself, cosmically speaking, mostly nothing and that might conclude senselessly in a smothering cloud of cow farts (as Elaine's father at one point predicts) or in the sun going supernova (Elaine's brother's more probable prediction), an ending with a bang a little louder but as empty quite.

These last questions bring in the third, and in some ways most important, literary version of seeing in the dark embedded in the novel, Dante's *Inferno*. *Cat's Eye* metaphorically begins by reenacting Proust, but it both begins and concludes by reenacting Dante as well. In other words, whereas the book's Proustian impetus is to recover lost time so that it can be narrated, its Dantean impetus is to make moral sense of that narration, to see, not only the life of a past otherwise lost in time, but also what was lost by living that life. Just as the debt to Proust is explicitly acknowledged in the text, so is the debt to Dante. "This is the middle of my life," Elaine observes early in the novel (13), thereby, as David Cowart points out, "echoing Dante's famous opening" of the *Inferno* with him at the middle of his life but the beginning of his journey (126). She sees herself as being caught on "the middle of a bridge" (13) half over a river (or a ravine), just as he saw himself as being lost in the middle of a dark wood of error. Moreover, the Virgin Mary who appears to save Elaine is a version of Dante's Beatrice who was herself a version of the Virgin Mary, and Elaine, at the very end of the novel seeing the stars as she flies home to Vancouver, is herself a version of Dante seeing the "beauteous shining of the Heavenly / . . . Stars" in the last lines of the *Inferno* as he emerges from his journey through hell and sets off on the next stage, up the mountain of *Purgatory* and into the heavens of *Paradise* (*Inferno* 34.142–43). The stars Elaine sees are different from Dante's stars and demonstrate only Stephen's conception of the universe, not the scope and working of God's plan for man. "Echoes of light, shining out of the midst of nothing," Elaine concludes in the last lines of the novel, "It's old light, and there's not much of it. But it's enough to see by" (421). There are other echoes here too — Dante's "shining," Shakespeare's "nothing" — and in those echoes of light, and of other bleak and visionary texts, we see that Elaine Risley, like another female painter, Lily Briscoe in Virginia Woolf's *To the Lighthouse*, has "had [her] vision" (310). It, too, is "not much." Perhaps not much is all that is possible at this point in history and literature, with all master narratives now questioned and decentred. But it is enough to see by — enough for Elaine to see her past life and what it might mean, and for the reader to see the implications of her seeing.

Critical Reception

Cat's Eye early elicited distinctly mixed reviews. In Canada, Dennis Duffy, for example, found the protagonist to be "another flattened heroine," a "professional victim" who was "no more credible as a painter than . . . as a participant in the life of her time." The novel seemed so steeped in forced and faked misery ("conveying the feeling that growing up in Toronto proved a trifle gloomier than holidaying at Auschwitz") that "not even a Unified Field Theory could redeem" it (14). In contrast, Sherrill Grace thought Elaine Risley's account of her childhood suffering represented "some of the finest writing in Atwood's *oeuvre*" (137) and judged the book to have a "depth" and "wisdom" in its "celebration of life and art" that went "well beyond" Atwood's earlier novels in a similar vein such as *Surfacing* and *Life Before Man* (138). For Grace, even Elaine's *Unified Field Theory* painting added to *Cat's Eye*'s effect, serving, first, to unify the novel, especially with respect to its feminist implications, and, second, to incorporate it into the field of Atwood's other writing, both fiction and poetry. The female protagonist, Grace points out, "is a compound of witch, goddess, Virgin, and seer; she is the source of mystery, threat, comfort, and power, a beneficent muse . . . a mother and a mirror of the psyche." As such, she is also a "figure . . . Atwood has evoked . . . before in the shape of the mother in *Surfacing*, the triple goddess in *Lady Oracle*, Circe in *You Are Happy*, and Moodie in *The Journals of Susanna Moodie*" (137).

In the United States, Rhoda Koenig, even more than Duffy, assessed the book as virtually meritless: "The writing is as flat, mean, and constipated as the content is perfunctory and banal, the morality smug." A computer plugged "into the bank labeled POSTWAR, PUBERTY, FEMALE (FICTION)," Koenig suggests, could surely be programmed to come up with "something more sprightly than *Cat's*

Eye" (81). (Whether *Cat's Eye* aims at sprightly, is, of course, another question.) Alison Lurie, however, judged the novel a "brilliant" exploration of the "darker side of childhood friendship" and of the problems of being female and an artist in the contemporary world (38). Again the assessments are so diametrically opposed that one might well wonder if the two reviewers had read the same book. Atwood, we know from one of her interviews, sometimes half-humorously asks if the Atwood work being reviewed is, indeed, the same one she wrote: "You find yourself looking under the sofa for some other book by the same name that might have strayed into the reviewer's hands by mistake" (Ingersoll, *Conversations* 238).

Of course, different readers are going to respond to the same text differently. One person's masterpiece is another's potboiler. What seems, for one, a brave new twist to a crucial story will be, for another, the same old previously assayed subject treated in the same old tired way. Atwood invites such a polarized response because with each new novel she both rewrites and doesn't rewrite her previous books. The new work, for some reviewers, will be déjà vu all over again. She did it better, or at least more originally, they will maintain, in *Surfacing*. For others, the difference will stand out, and this difference can also divide, can be seen as marking an advance or a falling away from the standard set by the previous novel or novels. In short, the deep split in the first reviewers' assessments of the quality of *Cat's Eye* is itself a measure of how hard it is to get a fix on a particular Atwood text and to decide just what she is attempting in the book.

The same split can be seen more specifically in opposing views regarding the novel's stance towards feminism. For some reviewers, such as Richard Bautch and William French, *Cat's Eye* is explicitly antifeminist in that it shows a woman suffering at the hands of other women. It is not just men, either, who see the novel as letting men off the hook. Alice McDermott detects in the book an "undercurrent of misogyny" (35), while Gayle Greene finds far more than an undercurrent. For Greene, the novel "is a tale not of human evil, but of female evil, from which males are generally absent and exempt, in which there is . . . a misogyny so pronounced and so unprocessed, that it is impossible to say whether it is Elaine's, society's, or Atwood's" (448). Grace, however, insists that the novel "is not rejecting feminism" (138), and Sharon Thompson similarly argues that it "is not misogynistic" but is instead "a critique of gender segregation and fundamentalist bigotry, not of being born female" (50). Other assessments fall between these poles. For Hermione Lee, *Cat's Eye* represents Atwood's disengagement from feminism, and for Shena Mackay it shows Atwood's basic scepticism towards "Sisterhood" and suggests that "she was always a co-opted rather than a card-carrying member of the North American Women's Movement" (113). Carole Cleavor even argues that the failure of the book lies in its angry and outdated feminism (19), while for Judith Thurman its failure lies in its unrealized antifeminism, its reluctance to foreground "a fierce, enthralling [drama] of [female] bondage . . . buried in a sprawling bildungsroman" (108), a drama that would show more clearly and convincingly a woman's "complicity" in her own victimization. If the quality of the novel is difficult to define, so, apparently, is the quality of its feminism.

The feminism or antifeminism of *Cat's Eye* will be assessed at greater length in the subsequent critical essays and book chapters and so will a number of other questions first raised by the reviewers, particularly the role of Cordelia, the implications of the novel's portrayal of little girls, the connections between the narrative present of the retrospective show in Toronto and Elaine's remembered childhood past, the symbolic significance of Elaine's paintings, the way Elaine herself is to be understood as an artist, and the place of the novel in Atwood's *oeuvre*. If the reviews were not very successful at telling us just how we should read what was then Atwood's latest book, they did do a better job at delineating the lines that would be profitably pursued in subsequent assessments of this text.

The summary charges of antifeminism and even misogyny which some reviewers early levelled against *Cat's Eye* have been substantially answered in subsequent and more sustained assessments. As a number of critics emphasize, feminist issues pervade the novel (see, for example, J. Brooks Bouson, Sonia Gernes, Coral Ann Howells, Judith McCombs, Eleanor Rao, Martha Sharpe, Hilde Staels, and Susan Strehle). Particularly good treatments of the feminist implications of the novel are Molly Hite's essay, "An Eye for an I: The Disciplinary Society in *Cat's Eye*," and the chapter, "*Cat's Eye* Vision: 'Rapunzel' and 'The Snow Queen,' " in Sharon Rose Wilson's *Margaret Atwood's Fairy-Tale Sexual Politics*. Hite employs Michel Foucault, and Wilson the two fairy tales in her chapter title as different intertexts through which to assess the novel, but their readings are suggestively similar. As Hite points out, "the discursive structure" of *Cat's Eye* emphasizes "the political implications of conventionally personal events" (191) and particularly the sexual politics of the power of the gaze, whereby women are "both [given] an identity and . . . identified as vulnerable" (195). The novel shows just how much women are "singled out for enforced visibility" (197), are subject to the guilt of being female, and are prompted to see themselves as in need of improvement and to police other women by pointing out their various imperfections. Under Cordelia's critical scrutiny, "Elaine learns to internalize the condemnatory gaze without discerning the means to 'improve' herself that will remove her from the range of such judgements" because "the goal of improvement is part of the mechanism of condemnation and as such is unrealizable" (195). As partial escapes from the losing game of being female, she tries to deny "her inclusion in the category 'woman' " (196) and to claim "as a painter . . . a position [of viewing subject] usually reserved for the dominant class of men in a patriarchal system" (197), but each of these escapes "also represents a deeply unsatisfying complicity with masculine institutions" (193). By the end of the novel, however, Elaine has come to reassess her life, her relationships with other women, and, most of all, the workings of a disciplinary society particularly committed to disciplining women. She can finally forgive her mother and Mrs. Smeath, Cordelia and herself, and can accept a feminist commitment to mercy represented by the Virgin as "above all an agent of restoration, a Virgin of Lost Things who redresses estrangement" (203), in place of a masculinist "ethics of personal culpability" and an old-testament insistence on "an eye for an eye" which "leads," in Hite's conclusion as well as Elaine's, "only to more blindness" (*Cat's Eye* 405; Hite 205). Hite also demonstrates how Stephen's death (like more minor episodes such as Elaine's street encounter with the refugee woman) serves to prompt Elaine's final awareness, and so counters those critics who deemed the brother's murder a "cheap" irony (Koenig 82) or a "glaring excrescence" (Banerjee 521).

Wilson charts much the same progression for the protagonist. In her view, Elaine, like other Atwood characters, "must recover feeling" and cultivate "an empathetic vision" rather than a narcissistic vision that plays tricks with mirrors. "In order to see rather than to reflect, [Atwood's protagonists] must stop being mirrors and using others as mirrors. They must remove the glass eyes of mirror or camera vision that alienate them from themselves, others, and the world" (298). More specifically, Elaine must overcome her "eye problems," particularly her reliance on her "unfeeling glass eye" cat's eye marble perspective (300). In so doing, she frees herself from her Rapunzel-like captivity in her repressed Toronto past and from the Snow Queen coldness that characterizes her relationships with others. By "send[ing] Cordelia 'home'" at the end of the novel and allowing her to be the subject of her own story rather than a mirror of Elaine's, Elaine can at last go home herself as "an 'I' with eyes and heart" (312–13). Wilson also emphasizes the feminist implications of this admittedly fairy-tale progression from captivity to release. "Atwood's fairy-tale intertexts not only depict patriarchal victimization of females: they foreground the amputations — of the senses, of selfhood, of relationship to the natural world, and of the protagonists' national and global community — inherent in phallocentric sexual politics" (313). Those politics, as Wilson points out, are made particularly obvious in the novel by the fake body parts that litter Jon's studio and by the fact that he is currently doing the special effects for a chain-saw massacre movie. But fairy tales, unlike "Friday-the-Thirteenth" and "Freddie" movies, model the way out of victimization and dismemberment as well as the way in. They show "the kind of 'magic' necessary to transform 'pre-human' individuals and societies into fully human ones. Remembering the possibility of transformation and speaking against all that would silence the human voice and art, Atwood's characters [such as Elaine] re-member their own symbolically dismembered bodies and re-vision the discredited old stories" (314).

As the above quotations suggest, Wilson's reading of *Cat's Eye* is all the more convincing in that it assesses the text not just through its fairy-tale intertexts but also in terms of how still other intertexts function in much the same fashion in all of Atwood's novels. Several other critics similarly incorporate their discussion of the feminist implications of *Cat's Eye* within a larger assessment of Atwood's career as a feminist author. Eleanor Rao, for example, in *Strategies for Identity: The Fiction of Margaret Atwood*, maintains that the novel represents the female subject as a provisional and shifting construct and, in her chapter "Writing the Female Subjects," stresses that in all her novels Atwood portrays "womanliness . . . as a mask, a disguise that stubbornly resists interpretation," even while she also depicts "the female subject's different forms of resistance" to masculine attempts to appropriate her subjectivity and dictate her desires (132). Making much the same argument in slightly different terms, J. Brooks Bouson, in *Brutal Choreographies: Oppositional Strategies and Narrative Design in the Novels of Margaret Atwood* (one of the best books yet on Atwood's fiction), gives a detailed and carefully nuanced reading of *Cat's Eye* as both an account and a critique of how "femininity is constructed in our culture" (166) and so shows how this novel, like its predecessors, "focuses attention on the power politics that govern women's lives [and] the patterns of domination and subordination that occur not only in heterosexual romance but also in mother-daughter relationships and in women's friendships" (10). Bouson also observes that the art of the novel serves partly to point out the limitations of art and thereby present "dark female anxieties . . . that art can never truly frame or control" (184). More recently, Coral Ann Howells, in *Margaret Atwood*, similarly concludes that one of the strengths of the novel is its refusal to delimit the female subject: "The best Elaine Risley or Margaret Atwood can offer is a Unified Field Theory from which inferences about the subject may be made, but the subject herself is always outside, in excess, beyond the figuration of language" (160). *Cat's Eye* thereby "highlight[s] . . . the artifice of representation" even as it provides another representation of Atwood's "most 'capacious topic' . . . the operation of power politics at every level" (162).

Unlike the first reviewers, most critics view *Cat's Eye* as a feminist novel, but that verdict is not unanimous. Lynn Crosbie, for example, in "Like a Hook into a *Cat's Eye*: Locating Margaret Atwood's Susie," faults Atwood for her antifeminist misrepresentation of Susie, the other young art student whose affair with the teacher precedes and then overlaps with Elaine's. Crosbie argues that Susie is portrayed "from a detached and pitiless perspective"; that she "is *silenced* and obscured in the text that is devoted to the notion of resurrection and revision"; and that this failure is the author's when Susie becomes finally "an aporia, an impassable path that Atwood can[not], or will not traverse" (31). However, this charge is not convincing. To start with, Atwood clearly presents the absence of sympathy for Susie's painful situation as Elaine's failure. So when Crosbie criticizes Atwood for not adequately recognizing the similarities between

Susie and Elaine, she can do so only by failing herself to recognize that it is Atwood who worked these similarities into the novel in the first place. Indeed, by having Elaine note her persistent problems with "twin sets" even as she is describing Susie's plight, Atwood pointedly emphasizes how Elaine's failure to see herself in Susie should be interpreted. Crosbie, in fact, observes that "Elaine does dream of Susie asking her if she knows what a 'twin set' is, but," she continues, "Atwood never returns to, or addresses, this provocative suggestion" (31). With the "suggestion" of denied twinship so obviously foregrounded, what further address is necessary?

Closely related to considerations of the feminist implications of the novel are assessments of the protagonist as a female artist and of the significance of her paintings, which are described at length in the text. Again, most critics argue for a feminist interpretation of Atwood's portrait of this woman painter and her art. Thus Judith McCombs, in "Contrary Re-memberings: The Creating Self and Feminism in *Cat's Eye*," points out how all the paintings, particularly those of Mrs. Smeath, express Elaine's girlhood, adolescent, and young adult anxieties about being female. McCombs further observes that the five paintings done during the year before the retrospective show and hung together on one wall all come after Elaine's "seeing her life entire in the cat's eye" and are themselves a "summing up" of her life (13–14). McCombs persuasively interprets each of these paintings and shows how they, like the earlier works, "stress . . . female experiences and female patterns of creativity" (14).

In a slightly different vein, Howells argues that the novel, through Elaine's narrative of her past and description of her paintings (which Howells, like McCombs, assesses in detail), presents a "double figuration of the self" (149). Howells notes that one half of that doubling is itself differently doubled when Elaine's account of what the paintings signify to her is contrasted to "the wickedly satirical extracts from the [retrospective art show] catalogue commentary." These different takes on Elaine and her paintings are, moreover, mirrored in the paintings themselves with "their pier-glass motifs or their triptych designs, which imitate shifts in perspective," and with their "different spatial patternings, different time dimensions, executed in different painterly techniques," through which "a host of possible meanings are generated" (158). In these "multiplicities" (158) of meaning the paintings become "sub-versions" (the name of the gallery holding the retrospective show) of Elaine's life, while Elaine is constituted as a female subject both "in excess" of "the figurations of language" (160) and, at the same time, "partial and provisional," someone through whose eyes "we have learned to see" while seeing only "half her face or her face 'defaced' " (159). Because of that failure "*Cat's Eye* is [for Howells] Atwood's most developed version of life-writing in the feminine" (149). Grace, in "Gender as Genre: Atwood's Autobiographical 'I,' " has similarly maintained that Elaine's final painting, " 'Unified Field Theory' . . . replicates the novel *Cat's Eye* and provides us with an alternate image of the autobiographical 'I' " to portray thereby a "gendered Self" in a way "that denies logical categories and teleological order and presents instead a cyclical, iterative, layered narrative that invites exploration rather than arrival" (202) — a narrative that is also, for Grace, Atwood's "most profound, satisfying and . . . 'complete' rendering of the autobiographical 'I' as a female Subject" (192). Martha Sharpe, too, in an essay on Atwood and Julia Kristeva, argues that "despite Elaine's . . . political distance from feminism," her "symbolization of her private experience in her paintings speaks volumes to other women" (174), and Susan Strehle, in *Fiction and the Quantum Universe*, stresses that "Elaine Risley becomes an artist committed to disrupting her culture's view of women" (175). Jessie Givner, in "Names, Faces and Signatures in Margaret Atwood's 'Cat's Eye' and 'The Handmaid's Tale,' " also assesses the paintings in some detail to see in them "a play between the half-face and the full-face" (67) that mirrors the novel's "uncanny play between doubles and halves, figuration and disfiguration" (66). For Givner, this play is also a feminist decentring of the subject and a textual exercise in "openness and plurality [that] provides an interesting intersection between [Atwood's] fiction and Luce Irigaray's feminist theory" (72). The argument is highly theoretical and abstruse, but its feminist implications are obvious.

Once again, however, there is a dissenting, and not very convincing, voice. Jacques LeClaire, in "Margaret Atwood's *Cat's Eye* as a Portrait of the Artist," argues that the paintings express "the romantic notion that art is born of the self, that it draws its energies from what is unique in the artist, together with the modern view that the work of art achieves independent life." In defence of this assessment, he quotes Elaine's description of her *Life Drawing* painting, which portrays a nude Josef and a nude Jon each painting differently a nude but draped woman with a sphere of blue glass for a head, and then concludes that Elaine "accounts for the elements present in the picture in apparently matter-of-fact references to incidents taken from her own life, and makes sure they cannot be given a feminist twist" (78). Other critics, however, have no problem at all in giving the painting a feminist twist. McCombs notes that the depiction of the nude male painters and the draped female model "both criticizes and comically reverses" the general gender prerogatives of just who gets to be dressed and who doesn't in Western art even as it also shows that "each man is painting his own culturally-oriented projection" of woman as cultural construct (15), as an objectified "other," a reflector and lens (the glass head) rather than as another thinking, feeling human being.

Other critical perspectives on particular features of the novel, such as its postcolonial implications or its employment of the miraculous, will be incorporated into my reading of Cat's Eye in the next chapter. I will here conclude my survey of the criticism by noting how a number of critics have placed the novel within a larger context, most commonly the context of Atwood's other novels. The work of Bouson, Rao, Staels, and Wilson to this end has already been noted. Howells's *Margaret Atwood* also evaluates the author's fiction to date and deems her "the best-known feminist writer in English" because of "her scrutiny of social myths of femininity; male and female fantasies about women; representations of women's bodies in art, fiction, popular culture and pornography; women's social and economic exploitation; as well as women's relations with each other, not to mention their relations with men" (163). This last quote could just as well represent an overview of Cat's Eye as of Atwood's entire *oeuvre*. Howells also observes that in Cat's Eye, as in all her works, "Atwood is writing time as she is writing women, writing Canada, mapping cultural shifts and changing fashions" (166). With less focus on Cat's Eye, Shannon Hengen, in *Margaret Atwood's Power: Mirrors, Reflections and Images in Select Fiction and Poetry*, has written a book-length "power politics" assessment of how Atwood portrays both Canada and women.

In a slightly different vein, Nathalie Cooke assesses Atwood's "fictive confessions," exploring how a number of novels, particularly *Lady Oracle, The Handmaid's Tale*, and Cat's Eye, employ the conventions of the confessional to encourage the reader to confront the ethical implications of a work. Lorraine York, in " 'Over All I Place a Glass Bell': The Meta-Iconography of Margaret Atwood," looks at how "all of [Atwood's] work to date" presents "a critique of iconization" (231) and how *Cat's Eye* especially does so, critiquing both the iconization of the artist and of her art, while also showing that Elaine's "artful, iconic" painting is superior to that of Jon in his search for style. He "fatuously excuses his own return to figural art by saying that he is using 'common cultural sign systems to reflect the iconic banality of our times,' " whereas "Elaine has discovered that icons — both contemporary and ancient — are anything but banal" (244).

Two critics, I would finally note, place *Cat's Eye* in a context other than Atwood's other works. Carol Beran, in "Images of Women's Power in Contemporary Canadian Fiction by Women," after considering novels and short-story collections by Atwood, Alice Munro, and Aritha van Herk, concludes that "Atwood's recent writings [*The Handmaid's Tale* and *Cat's Eye*] see the female's power in terms of her ability to voice her life and emotions," and so for Atwood and her protagonists "artistic creation becomes the symbol of women's greatest power" (75). Drawing on a still larger and more diverse body of fiction, sixteen novels written since 1967 (the year of Canada's centennial), Frank Davey assesses *Cat's Eye* to quite a different end. In *Post-National Arguments: The Politics of the Anglophone-Canadian Novel since 1967*, he argues that recent Canadian fiction fails to address the large political questions of how a national polity is constructed and depicts instead individual accommodations to an unexamined present, retreats to an overexamined past, or parables of success on a transnational level (the protagonists are as much at home in Europe or the United States as in Canada). For Davey, Elaine "has considerable awareness of the differences that she has possessed at various times in her life through being a girl, a woman, a stranger to urban life, and an artist," but she has "almost none of how she may have been different through being born Canadian" (233). Similarly, "the human Canada" Elaine inhabits at the end of the novel is "almost totally lacking in social codes and discourses" and "is an individual . . . rather than a public space" (238). *Cat's Eye*, Davey concludes, is one of the more politically positive novels of those he considers, and one of "only five . . . which openly resist the transnational," but he still finds it wanting: "The only symbol of resistance to the transnational the novel can offer is the cat's eye itself—the shining, 'crystalline,' mysteriously essential self" (260). Davey's is an interesting but I think fundamentally flawed reading of the novel. *Cat's Eye* is not about resisting the transnational, and to judge it by its failure in this enterprise is roughly comparable to condemning *Post-National Arguments* for not providing convincing feminist critiques of the novels assessed.

Reading of the Text

ON FIRST LOOKING INTO ATWOOD'S *CAT'S EYE*

The title, of course, is the reader's first clue as to what kind of a story a novel will tell. If that is what the author named it, that must be what she thinks it is about, and she, after all, wrote the book. But the title as a sign usually points to a way of approaching a text rather than simply declaring its contents, and Atwood has regularly demonstrated her preference for suggestively ambiguous titles (from *The Edible Woman* and *Surfacing* to *The Robber Bride* and *Wilderness Tips*) that can apply in different ways to the narratives they name. *Cat's Eye* fits this pattern.

To start with, the title can be taken literally or metaphorically. The metaphorical implications of being able to see in the dark are particularly apt, for much of the novel consists of the protagonist's re-visioning of her earlier life. By seeing into the darkness of times past, Elaine must also look into still other metaphoric darknesses, the "hearts of darkness" that practised (or, with the adults, countenanced or could not countermand) the childhood cruelty of Cordelia's original victimization of Elaine and then Elaine's subsequent victimization of Cordelia. Yet the literal implications fit, too. If we suspect that the novel could hardly be named after an anatomical part of a cat (analogous, say, to "cat's ear"), there are cat's eyes enough in the text and in the protagonist's paintings described in the text to dispel that doubt. Indeed, those eyes in the paintings looking out at the painter-protagonist, the author, and the reader all looking in constitute an example of Atwood's metafictional mirroring and another hint of how, as Atwood suggests in her early poem, "This is a Photograph of Me," the portrait of the portrayed is also a portrait of the portrayer (a point regularly made in the descriptions of Elaine's paintings) and even a portrait of the viewer. Moreover, "cat's eye" has a second and more central literal significance. Seeing the cat's eye marble saved from her childhood, a middle-aged Elaine recovers, in Proustian fashion, that whole past, and so much of the novel as an account of her childhood is, in effect, seen through a cat's eye.

Cat's Eye as a title also serves well in a second double sense. "Cat's eye" as in seeing or "cat's eye" as in dissecting? This question is all the more apt when we remember that it was her interest in zoology and zoological illustrations that first prompted Elaine to become a painter. Furthermore, the legacy of this unusual apprenticeship remains evident in her art, as is pointedly emphasized in some of her paintings, such as the portrait of Mrs. Smeath that tries to get to the heart of that cold woman by depicting her heart as the heart of a turtle Elaine once dissected and drew in a high-school biology class. To see Mrs. Smeath here is to cut her open, to figuratively kill her. The portrait foregrounds the power play of all portraiture, the cruelty of art. Torture, Atwood observes in "Notes Towards a Poem That Can Never Be Written," is "[p]artly . . . an art" (*Selected Poems II, 72*), and art, she suggests through the interplay of the implications of to see and to dissect even in the title of the novel, is partly a torture.

The torture of art versus the art of torture might seem to have taken us some distance from the simple designation "cat's eye." Yet the implications of this mirroring in the title are supported by more obvious mirrorings within the text. Elaine's treatment of Mrs. Smeath in the portrait, for example, reflects Mrs. Smeath's earlier treatment of Elaine. And Cordelia's cruelty, as will be discussed in more detail later, was premised on her "picture" of what Elaine was and of what Cordelia concomitantly was not — which is, of course, precisely what Cordelia was. Seeing as dissecting as not seeing! That third term in the sequence, and the possibility that much in life is not fully and clearly perceived, is also suggested by the significance of "cat's eye" as a marble, for a world viewed through a coloured glass sphere is necessarily radically distorted. In short, *Cat's Eye* as a title presages a world dark enough both literally (how to see the past) and figuratively (how to understand it) that the reader might well require cat's eyes to travel this fictional realm.

The novel's two epigraphs also serve as suggestive reading directives. The first, from Eduardo Galeano's *Memory of Fire: Genesis*, recounts how an old tribal woman survived her demise by continuing on in the souls of those who killed her:

When the Tukanas cut off her head, the old woman collected her own blood in her hands and blew it towards the sun.

"My soul enters you, too!" she shouted.

Since then anyone who kills receives in his body, without wanting or knowing it, the soul of his victim. (n.p.)

This epigraph most obviously refers to Elaine and Cordelia, who as victims of one another continue to survive in one another. More generally, the literal beheading in the epigraph recurs throughout the novel as the figurative dismembering of women. The old woman scattering her blood towards the sun in a final act of transcendent self-expression is also a correlative to Elaine as another woman artist surviving in and through her art. The old woman's triumph over death is a triumph over time as well, and so is suggestive of how time will be defeated in the novel too: through memory (the reclaiming of the past) and through art (the conserving of both the reclaimed past and the unfolding present).

But does time, as that previous sentence implies, consist of a present ever passing into the past, which brings us to the second of the two epigraphs: "Why," Stephen W. Hawking asks in *A Brief History of Time*, "do we remember the past, and not the future?" His title reminds us that time, too, has a history that merits recounting and is not the simple counting off of nanoseconds, hours, eons, whatever. As cosmologists since Einstein have pointed out, the universe is a time-space continuum in which the nature of both time and space are far from self-evident. Hawking himself is partly figured in the novel as the narrator's brother, Stephen, a cosmologist investigating how the universe might have taken shape in the first picoseconds of its creation. The working of time on the individual level (the structure of Elaine's narrative) is thus played out against the working of time on a cosmological level (the structure of the universe). We might also note here how the two epigraphs go together, mythology and cosmology both being attempts to assess how human beings exist in time.

* * *

Time is of the essence in the first sentence of the novel as well. "Time," the as yet unnamed narrator of *Cat's Eye* observes, "is not

34

a line but a dimension," and, like space, it too can be bent. So "if you knew enough and could move faster than light you could travel backward in time and exist in two places at once" (3). The novel itself immediately occupies those two places, but does so without the benefit of warp speed. In the narrative present Elaine remembers that it was her brother who told her of the fluidity of time, and as she does so she also vividly remembers that brother "when he wore his ravelling maroon sweater to study in and spent a lot of time standing on his head so that the blood would run down into his brain and nourish it." She did not then "understand what he meant. . . . He was already moving away from the imprecision of words" (3). He subsequently moved still further away, we presently discover, into the silence of death, yet his teaching and his memory remain.

The interplay of present and past, of different pasts, is here especially grounded in the precision of Elaine's — and, behind her, Atwood's — words. Stephen's unravelling sweater, for example, foreshadows his later work on cosmological string theory, work he comes to doubt just before his death. His standing on his head anticipates a subsequent and more drastic reversal when he is the airplane passenger selected by the hijackers for execution. The blood that early "runs down" harmlessly will later, when he is thrown from the plane, do so in deadly earnest. In a different context, Elaine's early postulation "of time as having a shape" through the interplay of different memories, "like a series of liquid transparencies, one laid on top of another," anticipates the shape of the novel with its structuring principle of juxtaposed memories. There is also a characteristic Atwood ploy at the very beginning of *Cat's Eye*. "Sometimes," Elaine observes of these overlaid memories, "this comes to the surface, sometimes that." What also necessarily surfaces here for any reader who knows Atwood's earlier fiction is *Surfacing*. The overlaying of memories in the novel is thus also an overlaying of texts, which is to say that for Atwood as the author, as much as for Elaine as the protagonist, "nothing," in the last words of the first chapter, "goes away" (3).

"Nothing goes away." This fact is registered even in the titles of the novel's fifteen sections. They are all named after Elaine's paintings, and all of them except *Iron Lung*, the title of the first section, are described in the text as largely drawn from Elaine's past. But the opening section is also obviously a foray into the past. After the account of Stephen's disquisition on time/space, Elaine remembers herself and Cordelia at thirteen and Cordelia's derisive dismissal — " 'So?' " — of Stephen's views. Then, after also remembering how harshly they judged everyone else, especially older women, and noting what she has become and wondering what Cordelia might now think of her own aging body, Elaine, back in Toronto for her retrospective art show, fantasizes four possible meetings with her old "friend." Elaine has already undercut claims of friendship when she noted that the two thirteen-year-old girls "think [they] are friends" (4), and the fantasy reencounters do so more dramatically. She imagines, in quick succession, meeting Cordelia as a bag lady, witnessing her being assaulted in the street, being summoned to the hospital bedside of a dying Cordelia and "wondering whether to pull . . . the plug," and, "[e]ven better" (7), seeing Cordelia in an iron lung "being breathed, as an accordion is played. . . . fully conscious, but unable to move or speak" (8). Elaine then goes on to contemplate a more probable meeting, one not so obviously a projection of her anger from the past, and admits that if she actually did encounter Cordelia she doesn't know whether she would hug her "[o]r take her by the shoulders, and shake and shake" (8). What she does do is take long walks and begin "to chew [her] fingers again." In her words: "There's blood, a taste I remember. It tastes of orange popsicles, penny gumballs, red licorice, gnawed hair, dirty ice" (9).

The signs of the past are ominous — polio, penny candies that taste of blood. Even the idea of meeting Cordelia again causes Elaine such substantial mental pain that she reifies and redirects it through self-inflicted bodily pain, just as she did in the past. This partial merging of Elaine as an adult with Elaine as a child is also a partial merging of Elaine and Cordelia, for she inflicts on herself a version of the different suffering Cordelia once inflicted on her. Moreover, when Elaine walks the streets of Toronto, she becomes a version of Cordelia as the bag lady, and when, while walking, she feels her "throat tightening" (9), she similarly becomes a version of Cordelia being breathed in the iron lung, just as, chewing her fingers, she is Cordelia attacked in the street. In short, in a city still haunted by how she remembers it from the past — the "flat, dowdy, shabby-genteel" downtown she recalls played off against contemporary Toronto's "huge oblong towers, all of glass, lit up, like enormous gravestones of cold light" — she too is haunted by memories of the past. The contemporary towers through which "frozen assets" (8) achieve expression are, moreover, versions of iron lungs standing on end, and Elaine views herself as a woman still trapped in her past and living in and through that past. Memory itself is a metaphoric iron lung.

Or at least Elaine sees it this way. The first section also clearly evokes the questions on perspective implicit in the novel's title and epigraphs. Remembering her and Cordelia's contemptuous notice of older women's "blotchy" rouge, botched lipstick, and eyeliner eyes "drawn screw-jiggy around their real eyes," Elaine thinks that maybe these women "just couldn't see what they looked like." She herself now has "eye problems" and regularly wonders "what kind of modern art [she's] drawing on [her]self." Standing "too close to the mirror," she is "a blur, too far back and [she] can't see the details." The mirror here reflects the functioning of memory. Furthermore, even when Elaine gets "the distance adjusted," she can still "vary" and "some days . . . look like a worn-out thirty-five, others like a sprightly fifty. So much depends on the light, and the way you squint" (5). When you are in an iron lung, however, it is hard to control how far you are from the mirror or the direction from which the light falls. In the chapters that follow, the nature of that metaphoric iron lung will be made clearer, as will Elaine's determination to come to terms with and to free herself from the past that still holds her.

The drab Toronto of her childhood is superimposed against the trendy financial capitol of Canada to which she returns for her retrospective art show. Yet in other ways, too, Elaine regularly plays off details from the present against her memories of the past in order to see who she is, was, and how far she has come, which often turns out to be a rather shorter distance than might at first appear to be the case. For example, the second section, "Silver Paper," begins: "I'm lying on the floor, on a futon, covered by a duvet. *Futon, duvet*: this is how far we've come" (13). Camped out in her ex-husband's studio, she at first sees futons and duvets as signs of how much the world has changed. But when, in much of this section, she remembers her nomadic early childhood with her entomologist father, camped out in the bush or staying in motels and temporary winter apartments, we notice that sleeping on the floor in a place not her own is, in a sense, "coming home" for Elaine. This point is also partly made by the fact that it is her ex-husband's studio and by the consideration that she also presently sleeps with him again too — and on the floor, just as they did the first time.

Elaine herself also immediately denies the difference that she just asserted. The passage just quoted from the opening of the second section continues:

> I wonder if Stephen ever figured out what futons and duvets were. Most likely not. Most likely if you'd said *futon* to him, he'd have looked at you as if he was deaf or you were brain-damaged. He did not exist in the futon dimension.
>
> When there were no futons and no duvets, the price of an ice-cream cone was five cents. Now it's a dollar if you're lucky, and not as big either. That's the bottom-line difference between then and now: ninety-five cents. (13)

But the difference is clearly more than that: a nostalgic lament for a time when "prices" were lower. As the suffering implicit in Elaine's memories attests — "I hate this city," she soon acknowledges — the price was higher in childhood, and it was paid in pain, not in pennies.

Elaine's attempt to reduce the difference between then and now to "ninety-five cents," the angst-laden tone of her memories, and the structure of her thinking (which is the structure of the book — the continued juxtaposition of what she remarks on in her present with what she remembers from her past) all attest to how she has not yet come to terms with that past and who she consequently is, how she is still lost in a long-repressed dark world of childhood. That same point is suggested early in the second section by the evocation of Dante's *Inferno*. Elaine in "the middle of [her] life," which she sees "as a place, like the middle of a river, the middle of a bridge, halfway across, halfway over," suggests Dante at the beginning of the *Inferno* similarly lost in the middle of his life and in the middle of the dark wood of error, just as Elaine "dragged downwards, into the layers of this place [Toronto] as into liquefied mud" (13), corresponds to Dante making his descent through a multilayered hell. But he completed both his journeys — through the dark woods and through hell — and so can she. A bridge, in fact, is precisely what she needs to get over the mud, and, in this context, the *Inferno* itself functions in *Cat's Eye* as a kind of metaphoric bridge marking the way that a crossing might be made.

The novel, as R.D. Lane has argued at length, specifically evokes Shakespeare's *King Lear*. Cordelia is named after that king's youngest daughter, and when she is first remembered in interaction with Elaine (as opposed to just being remembered), the action is an obvious reference to *King Lear*: "*What do you have to say for yourself?* Cordelia used to ask. *Nothing*, I would say. It was a word I came to connect with myself, as if I was nothing, as if there was nothing there at all" (41). Cordelia's crucial "nothing" in the play, in response to her father's insistence that she expand more fulsomely on her love for him, leads to his statement "[n]othing will come of nothing" (1.1.92–95), his act of disinheriting her, and the subsequent tragedy that befalls them both. Atwood, in effect, doubly reverses *King Lear*. The "nothing" the king gives to Cordelia in the play is, in the novel, given by Cordelia to Elaine, and the concomitant question is not so much what will come of that nothing, but from what did that nothing come.

It comes, mostly, and this is one of the main points of *Cat's Eye*, from the fact that Elaine is a girl and from the way she tries to accommodate herself to the social ramifications of having been born female. These ramifications are introduced early in the novel through the wilderness/city polarity that Atwood has deployed and deconstructed in her fiction from *Surfacing* to *Wilderness Tips*. It is therefore important to look at the symbolic significance of the north woods where Elaine lived with her brother, as opposed to Toronto where she finally acquires the "girl" friends she has long suspected she requires. For Elaine, the woods were a place of freedom, not of error. In her nomadic childhood she was substantially exempt from social and gender restraints and played freely with her one older brother at games more prototypically "male" than "female" — pretend war rather than pretend housekeeping (but mostly played, it must be admitted, in the roles he assigned her). Error lay in the city. It was there that she felt she had to become a proper girl and was nearly killed in the process of being made into one, which is why she continues to hate the city and why her return to Toronto evokes so many painful memories from her past. But of course Atwood also makes it clear that matters are more complicated than this simple dichotomy suggests. The problems of being female in a sexist society are not solved by leaving the urban world for a life of freedom in the forest. That wasn't a real option at the conclusion of *Surfacing*, and neither is it at the beginning of *Cat's Eye*.

"Up north, the young Elaine" was not in the "state of grace" Stephen Ahern has postulated (9). To start with, the city partly penetrates the forest. The children weren't totally free. Schooling was still mandatory, and their mother taught them both, using a standard school reader, "about two children who live in a white house with ruffled curtains, a front lawn, and a picket fence. The father goes to work, the mother wears a dress and an apron, and the children play ball on the lawn with their dog and cat. Nothing in these stories is anything like my life," Elaine observes at the time (29). "There are no tents, no highways, no peeing in the bushes, no lakes, no motels. There is no war. The children are always clean, and the little girl, whose name is Jane, wears pretty dresses and patent-leather shoes with straps." The example of Jane is present even if Jane is not, though of course this picture-perfect Jane is not regularly encountered in the city either. Nevertheless, she has an "exotic appeal" for Elaine who soon begins to "draw girls" rather than her brother's "ordinary wars." She "draw[s] them in old-fashioned clothing, with long skirts, pinafores and puffed sleeves, or in dresses like Jane's, with big hairbows on their heads," and thus registers "the elegant, delicate picture [she has] in [her] mind, about other little girls" (29). Such drawing is an apprenticeship in art and an early indication that Elaine will become a painter. It is an apprenticeship in being female as well, in achieving through the right air and attire the socially expected elegance and delicacy that "becomes" a girl. It is thus also an apprenticeship in nothingness, for in seeking to portray what she thinks she should be, Elaine concomitantly registers how much she falls short of the ideal and how she is therefore somehow lacking. In the supposed freedom of the forest, she well knows of the larger social world elsewhere and of what that world wants her to be. Indeed, even while playing dead in her brother's war games, Elaine is enacting two features of that larger world, its penchant for massive deployments of lethal force and its gendering of power and politics.

When her father gives up his job as a forest entomologist and moves, with his family, to the city to become a professor of biology, Elaine finds, as his new profession attests, that forest and city interpenetrate in the city as well as in the forest. Toronto's ravines, for example, can be seen as a forest foray into an urban setting. Also suggestive are the mice kept in the basement of the botany building where her father teaches and where Elaine regularly goes with her brother to play before she has acquired her longed-for girl friends. There she is told that if you put a "strange mouse . . . with the wrong, alien scent" into a cage with other mice, "they will bite it to death" (36). She will soon discover that this animal behaviour from the cellar, so to speak, is not that different from what her friends will do to her in their homes, at school, and on the streets of the city, and in the ravine as well.

Moved to the city, the family at first still camps out. Their house is not finished; wires dangle where light fixtures should be; everything is missing in the kitchen except the sink; "[n]othing is painted"; there is "an enormous hole" in the yard; and the whole place is "surrounded by raw mud" (32). They still sleep on the floor and eat off a card table. Elaine's first friend, Carol Campbell, after visiting, "tells everyone at school" of these actions "as if she's reporting on the antics of some primitive tribe" (49). This report both betrays Elaine and marks her as different. The new home was not completed because the contractor had gone bankrupt, which perhaps suggests some bankruptcy in the social contract as well, particularly with respect to women and the domestic life to which they are ostensibly consigned. The hole in the ground also foreshadows another hole in another yard, Cordelia's hole in which Elaine will be buried, just as, as a version of nothing, it also anticipates the "nothing" to which she will herself soon be reduced. No wonder that Elaine, contemplating this ominously unfinished house, "want[s] to be back in the motel, back on the road, in [her] old rootless life of impermanence and safety" (33), even though, as we have already seen, that life wasn't entirely safe either.

Elaine soon acquires the girl friends she thought she should have and begins to learn what is expected of her as a girl, even though she doesn't really understand the game of gender as it is played out in the city and particularly at her school. She notices how the playground is rigorously sexually segregated and how the segregation symbolically extends to the rest of school. For her, it makes no sense that there are separate "grandiose" GIRLS and BOYS entrances to a building in which they all end up in the same classrooms or that students supposedly "get the strap" if they go in through the wrong entrance

(45). "How," she asks, "is going in through a door different if you're a boy?" (46).

The difference is partly demonstrated by another form of schooling. When Elaine acquires a second friend, Grace Smeath, the three girls play school, with Grace "always the teacher," or they "sit on the floor in Grace's room with piles of old Eaton's Catalogues" and cut out a female figure and then supply their "lady" with everything they think she requires (53). As they each paste their lady with her "cut-out" possessions into a scrapbook, one catalogue is, in effect, made into another that is more condensed, more gendered, and more personal. Partly as a heritage of her different nomadic past, Elaine finds little appeal in the game; she contemplates "all these objects, these possessions that would have to be taken care of, packed, stuffed into cars, unpacked. . . . But Carol and Grace," she goes on to observe, "have never moved anywhere. Their ladies live in a single house and have always lived there" (53–54). Consequently, "[t]hey can . . . stuff the pages of their scrapbooks with dining room suites [no eating off the card table], beds [no sleeping on the floor], stacks of towels, one set of dishes after another, and think nothing of it" (54). Elaine also tellingly remembers that she has "seen lots of Eaton's Catalogues before: up north they're hung in outhouses for use as toilet paper," so they "remind [her] of the stench of such outhouses" (53), and she is occasionally dubious about the desires she is called on to share. Registering, for example, the "awe" with which Carol says "*chintz*" in describing her own living room furniture, Elaine thinks the word "sounds like the name of a kind of crayfish, or of one of the aliens on my brother's distant planet" (48); similarly, she is "disappointed" when Mrs. Campbell's vaunted and mysterious "twin set" turns out to be merely a pair of matched sweaters (50–51).

Despite some doubts, Elaine succumbs to the appeal of the image she is told she should embody. As she concludes in her description of the catalogue game: "I begin to want things I've never wanted before: braids, a dressing-gown, a purse of my own. Something is unfolding, being revealed to me. I see that there's a whole world of girls and their doings that has been unknown to me, and that I can be part of it without making any effort at all." The purpose of the game is perturbing and so are its rules: "I don't have to keep up with anyone, run as fast, aim as well, make loud explosive noises, decode messages, die on cue. I don't have to think about whether I've done these things well, as well as a boy. All I have to do is sit on the floor and cut frying pans out of the Eaton's Catalogue with embroidery scissors, and say I've done it badly. Partly this is a relief" (54). But doing badly is not doing well, no matter how you cut it. Her relief, moreover, will be short-lived. With the advent of Cordelia, Elaine will regularly be told that she does everything badly and will, indeed, be called on to do, both in play and in earnest, most of those things she has just claimed she is exempt from, right down to dying on cue.

One last loaded passage presages the role Cordelia will play in Elaine's life and that is the account of their first encounter. After another summer in the north woods where her father gleefully studied a classic infestation of tent caterpillars and "turned back into himself" (65), and where she and her brother reverted to their previous childhood selves, Elaine finds, on her return to Toronto, that her two friends have been joined by a third girl, who is taller, more attractive, and much more poised. The three watch Elaine and her family arrive back and begin to unpack, "as if [they were] new people, as if [she had] never lived here" (69). Although Carol and Grace presently deign to wave, they remain with Cordelia, standing apart, in the apple trees next to Elaine's house. Elaine is "conscious of [her] grubbiness, [her] unbrushed hair" (70), of how she and her family must appear to these three and particularly to Cordelia's measuring, amused surveillance. Then, when she walks over to the other girls, it is the third one, whom she doesn't know, who first speaks:

> "There's dog poop on your shoe," Cordelia says.
> I look down. "It's only a rotten apple."
> "It's the same colour though, isn't it?" Cordelia says. "Not the hard kind, the soft squooshy kind, like peanut butter." This time her voice is confiding, as if she's talking about something intimate that only she and I know about and agree on. She creates a circle of two, takes me in. (71)

Being taken in will also entail being taken, and there are two hints here of what is to come. The first is the false charge of "there's dog poop on your shoe," which anticipates how regularly Cordelia will soon be telling Elaine of other faults equally dubious and of how much Elaine, despite the injustice of the various charges, will be "in the shit," so to speak. The second hint is what that first "shit" actually was. A fallen rotten apple evokes another story of an apple, a fall, and a supposed source of rottenness in the world, and thus reminds us of a long-standing Western tradition for blaming a particular woman and holding her personally responsible for all that is generally wrong with life.

* * *

The games Elaine and her brother play in the north woods and before the family moves to Toronto are hardly innocent. They are mainly games of war. World War II regularly comes "filter[ing] in over the radio, remote and crackly," and is also evident closer at hand, in the "wooden guns, and daggers and swords" that Stephen makes, "with blood coloured onto the blades with red pencils" (24). Elaine, in learning to play dead, is learning to play the victim in other games to come. However, in an episode related to the book's title, she does gain something positive from Stephen's war games. At one point he teaches his sister "to see in the dark, as commandos do" by remaining "still" while "waiting until your eyes become accustomed to no light." Presently, "alone with [her] heartbeat and [her] too-loud breathing," she discovers "he's right: now [she] can see in the dark." Stephen also observes that you "never know when you might need" this skill (26). He is right there, too, for the whole novel attests to how the protagonist needs cat's eyes to see into the darkness of the pain and the past that she will years later narrate.

Elaine's early association with Cordelia also evokes, more literally, cat's eyes, just as it involves playing dead too and draws interconnections between vision and violence as well. As the four girls walk home from school, they load their pockets with horse chestnuts. The boys throw these spiked missiles at one another but the girls don't because "they could put out your eye" (74). They then cross over a ravine and a stream that "flows right out of the cemetery." Cordelia insists the water is "made of dissolved dead people" who might "come out of the stream, all covered with mist, and take you with them" (75). The girls leave these dead people a propitiatory meal of flowering weeds, horse chestnuts (themselves mildly poisonous), and more poisonous nightshade berries picked from along the edge of the path through the ravine. "The nightshade smells of earth, damp, loamy,

44

pungent, and of cat piss. Cats prowl around in there, we see them every day, crouching, squatting, scratching up the dirt, staring out at us with their yellow eyes as if we're something they're hunting" (74). Cats hunting you correspond to the dead who might also seize you as their prey, which gives quite a different meaning to cat's eyes and seeing in the dark. Other details of the scene are similarly ominous. The poison berries "red as valentine candies" (74) look back to the red licorice whips and orange popsicles that the girls shared just before finding the horse chestnuts and still further back in the text of the novel (but forward in time) to those same candies that evoked, Elaine remembers, like gnawed hair and dirty ice, the taste of blood. Poison as candy (death as temptation?) and the taste of blood anticipate Elaine's attempted suicide by slashing her wrists, which is itself a version of gnawing her fingers until the blood flows.

The flow of blood, furthermore, can signify differently for girls than for boys with their war play. The four girls, led by Cordelia, presently engage in "a lot of speculation about [the] underwear . . . of the female teachers," who, as unmarried women "over a certain age," have "something strange and laughable about" them (77). They imagine what different underwear the different women might wear and, in the case of one particularly unpopular teacher, not wear. Miss Lumley happily straps students herself rather than send them to the principal; as a proponent of the British Empire, she values England and the English more than Canada and Canadians. In retaliation, the students imagine her removing a pair of navy-blue wool bloomers at the back of the classroom every day. Elaine presently conflates the bloomers with Empire and "can't draw the Union Jack or sing 'God Save the King' without thinking about them." More perceptively, she also notes how she is connected with Miss Lumley:

I'm not afraid of snakes or worms but I am afraid of these bloomers. I know it will be the worse for me if I ever actually catch sight of them. They're sacrosanct, at the same time holy and deeply shameful. Whatever is wrong with them may be wrong with me also, because although Miss Lumley is not what anyone thinks of as a girl, she is also not a boy. When the brass handbell clangs and we line up outside our GIRLS door, whatever category we are in also includes her. (81)

Elaine's fear is of the adult female body and adult female sexuality. The "holy" (the clearly Freudian pun counters even as it foreshadows the "appearance" of the Virgin Mary) is played off against "deeply shameful" (menstruation and sex and babies born of conceptions less than immaculate). Elaine is not at all sure that she wants to go through that GIRLS door if it leads to being a Miss Lumley.

The girls' play soon becomes still more threatening. The day after Hallowe'en she and her three friends throw their jack-o'-lanterns off the bridge over the ravine to watch "them smash open on the ground below" (106), a foreshadowing of another fall to come. Cordelia then digs a big hole behind her house, supposedly for a clubhouse. This November digging that follows Hallowe'en, the night of the return of the dead, is followed by Remembrance Day, with its recitation of one of Canada's best-known poems, John McCrae's "In Flanders Fields." Hints of death abound, and, indeed, Elaine, recalling "We are the Dead," tries "to feel pious and sorry for the dead soldiers" but cannot because she has "never known any dead people" (107). Consistent with this thematics of death, what was to be a playhouse soon turns, instead, into a play grave, and the play grave, ominous enough in itself (Elaine is "supposed to be Mary Queen of Scots, headless already" [107] — and executed, it should be noted, on the orders of another woman, her cousin, Queen Elizabeth) turns figuratively real. Buried, covered over with boards and then with dirt, Elaine is left too long: "When I was put into the hole I knew it was a game; now I know it is not one. I feel sadness, a sense of betrayal. Then I feel the darkness pressing down on me; then terror." Yet in the narrative present Elaine admits that her understandable reactions to the horror of being buried alive are reconstituted, not real, memories: "When I remember back to this time in the hole, I can't really remember what happened to me while I was in it. I can't remember what I really felt. Maybe nothing happened, maybe these emotions I remember are not the right emotions." She knows that "after a while" she was retrieved from the hole and "the game or some other game continued." But she has "no image of [her]self in the hole; only a black square filled with nothing, a square like a door" (107).

To be so betrayed by one's friends and to be buried alive is to be reduced to the "nothing" that in Elaine's reconstruction filled the hole. The pain and trauma inflicted are overwhelming, and dissociation is one partial protection available to someone subject to such an assault. As nothing, Elaine need feel nothing; nothing bad can be done to nothing. With this nothing that signifies nothing, the adult Elaine splits herself off from the buried child Elaine, which is to say that although she can admit the other's suffering, she still cannot emotionally internalize it as her own. But this "nothing," it must also be emphasized, is not just Elaine's construct. It is even more Cordelia's. The relief that dissociation here provides therefore comes at a high price, for partial escape from the game that Cordelia plays serves, simultaneously, as a full admission of Elaine's defeat, as an acknowledgement that Cordelia has turned her into the nothing that is the goal of the game.

However, there is more at issue here than the suffering children can inflict on one another and the way in which Elaine as an adult still partly denies this episode from her past. The black square of nothing that is also a door recalls the GIRLS door at the school, which figuratively becomes the door through which Elaine did not want to go to become an adult woman. In much the same vein, the hole itself can be seen as a literalizing of the Freudian "holy" bloomers pun that renders woman as lacking, as nothing, and as appropriately consigned to nothing. In this context, to be female is to be figuratively dead, to be buried beneath the weight of social expectations of what a proper woman should and should not be. The game of criticizing Elaine, along with the earlier catalogue cut-out game, are both games of constructing a female identity that involve even more deadly deconstructions. As such, they appropriately converge in the grave. A girl escapes becoming a woman only if she dies as a girl, an end of play that a buried Elaine graphically embodies.

There is yet another analogue in the text to death play as a black hole of nothingness as a kind of door or entrance. In Stephen's cosmological terms, a black hole, of course, is the largest possible measure of nothingness and, on that large level, it also invites you, your planet, your solar system, perhaps even your whole galaxy to come on in and share in its nothingness. But, paradoxically and in another context, looking at nothing on the level of the universe can be at least partly reassuring. The novel regularly reminds readers that all the stars we see are "echoes" from the past because of the time it has taken for their light to reach us. They are no longer where and what they appear to be, yet they still shed light. Furthermore and on a lower cosmological level — the solar system rather than intergalactic space — Hallowe'en and Remembrance Day and the pretend burial are all described in terms of darkening streets, shortening days, and disappearing light. But "the weak November sunshine" (107) that pervades the late fall of this particular year will brighten in the spring, for that, too, is in the nature of stars and their planets and their light.

The implications of the turning year are not entirely positive, for it is the passing of years that will turn Elaine into the woman she doesn't want to become. Atwood gives Elaine the author's own November birthday to suggest much the same point by linking the birthday with Hallowe'en and Remembrance Day, which both commemorate death rather than life. The November birthday party is similarly juxtaposed with the November play burial, and, for Elaine, the two in retrospect are strikingly similar in that she reconstructs her memory of her party just as she does her memory of her interment and to much the same end of avoiding emotional pain: "There must have been a cake, with candles and wishes and a quarter and a dime wrapped in wax paper hidden between the layers for someone to chip a tooth on, and presents" (108). Even the quarter and the dime in the cake (another perfect detail that those of us who celebrated childhood birthdays in the fifties will remember) are, for Elaine, hypothetical and a danger. The "only trace" her parties have left is her continuing "vague horror of birthday parties, not other people's, [but her] own." At the very thought of "pastel icing" and "pink candles burning in the pale November afternoon light," she still feels "a sense of shame and failure" (108). In the narrative present, she closes her eyes to "wait for pictures . . . to fill in the black square of time" of the birthday she does not remember. The picture that comes, in contrast to the pastel and pink of the cake, is a profusion of tangled vines, "dark-green leaves with purple blossoms, dark purple, a sad rich colour, and clusters of red berries, translucent as water. . . . *Nightshade*, [she] think[s]," and even the word is "dark." She can "tell" that this is "the wrong memory," but it "persist[s], rich, mesmerizing, desolate, infused with grief" (108). The fading light of the November day and the small candles of the cake both sink into the darkness of night and the still darker nightshade, whose poison berries counter the cake as sustaining food, as the celebration of being born. The "black square of time" lost, the memories she has forgotten as a kind of dark door seems to open onto a future of only death. But

48

again, there are small signs of hope. The nightshade, Elaine notes, "is related to the potato." The red berries of the nightshade also suggest the eyes of the "unseen cats" evoked in the same passage, and cat's eyes can see in the dark.

The play of the text, the calculated juxtaposition of different details, perspectives, and times, introduces a note of hope or at least humour. This occurs in yet another context when, immediately after failing to remember her ninth birthday, Elaine, in the narrative present, notices that she has eaten all the food that Jon left and goes shopping. As she looks for the food section in a downtown department store, she is sprayed with "some venomous new perfume" ("venom" recalling the poison berries of the nightshade) that "smells like grape Kool-Aid" (a suggestion of a children's party). Then she finds herself "wading through rack after rack of children's party dresses" (113). This covert reference to *Macbeth* — "I am in blood / Stepped in so far that, should I wade no more, / Returning were as tedious as go o'er" (3.4.168–70) — is soon made more explicit. "[M]any of [the dresses] are in plaid" — even, suggestively, Black Watch (seeing in the dark?) plaid — which prompts a question: "Have these people forgotten history . . . don't they know any better than to clothe small girls in the colours of despair, slaughter, treachery, and murder?" But plaid, Elaine goes on to recall, "was the fashion in [her] day too. The white socks, the Mary Janes, the always-inadequate birthday present swathed in tissue paper, and the little girls with their assessing eyes, their slippery deceitful smiles, tartaned up like Lady Macbeth." Wading through party dresses, however, is not wading through gore, just as a little girl in a plaid dress at a birthday party is hardly Lady Macbeth, no matter how deceitful her smile. Although Elaine at this point vividly recalls the pain of her past — "In the endless time when Cordelia had such power over me, I peeled the skin off my feet" (113) — she can make progress in the present. An older saleslady, in contrast to the girl who sprayed her with the venomous perfume (and to Cordelia as a girl), finds Elaine "fingering" plaid dresses, afraid that she might be "slid[ing] off [her] trolley tracks in the middle of Simpsons Girlswear," and "kindly . . . directs" her to where she wants to go (115).

The department store setting is suggestive. Elaine is in Simpsons, a national department store that, like Eaton's, puts out its own catalogue; she is even in a Simpsons right next to "where Eaton's used to be" (111). Both the store and its setting recall the earlier Eaton's Catalogue game that was superseded by Cordelia's cataloguing of Elaine's faults, also just recalled by Elaine's memory of peeling her feet. That catalogue game, in its first form, did not survive the advent of Cordelia. "She knows, instantly it seems, why Grace's house has so many Eaton's Catalogues in it," for she is aware of the déclassé nature (in the fifties) of catalogue shopping, with its serviceable products, low prices, and limited choices (92). The making of a "lady" in the commercial sense through the simple accumulation of merchandise is transposed to a less material register; the lady is made by being given the right qualities and characteristics, which, of course, also entails taking away the wrong ones. This has its analogue in the material world of consumerism where, for instance, those lumpy wool coats bought from the catalogue just will not do. In both cases, the game has no real end or conclusion. Whatever one has is never enough; whatever one is is never enough either. That last point is effectively made in the novel when Elaine is criticized equally for first answering correctly all the questions on the Sunday Bible quiz (being a " 'goody-goody' "), and then, with the next quiz, deliberately getting some of them wrong (" 'She's getting stupider,' Cordelia says. . . . 'You'll have to try harder than that!' " [124]).

The social construction of woman in a patriarchal society is much like her material construction in a capitalist society. In each case nothing is enough. There is a fundamental lack that can never be adequately compensated for, a hole (and, as already noted, holes figure prominently in the text and in both their Freudian and Lacanian senses) that can never be filled in (much less expanded upon to become a penis or a phallus). The interconnection of the two constructions is also made doubly clear in the novel after Elaine is selected by her friends as the "lady" to be made over (the cosmetic implications of this term are regularly emphasized too, as when Elaine, in the present, is sprayed with perfume). First, Elaine continues the old cut-out game after the others have given it up, but now she cuts figures from women's magazines such as *Good Housekeeping* which show what women are to do with what the catalogues show them they are to own. That endless doing and owning also shows the hopelessness of the whole game of being perfect and thus the hopelessness of Elaine's present predicament, in which she takes a wry comfort:

I see that there will be no end to imperfection, or to doing things the wrong way. Even if you grow up, no matter how hard you scrub, whatever you do, there will always be some other stain or spot on your face or stupid act, somebody frowning. But it pleases me somehow to cut out all these imperfect women, with their forehead wrinkles that show how worried they are, and fix them into my scrapbook. (138)

These cut-out, imperfect women can be subjected, of course, to further editing. If the faces of particular figures that go in her scrapbook (itself a suggestive designation) do not appeal, Elaine "cut[s] off the heads and glue[s] other heads on" (138). That cutting mirrors her own plight — the way she is being cut down in order to measure up, which is itself mirrored in her own peeling of her feet. Second and equally suggestive, the remaking game is played partly in terms of the earlier catalogue game. Elaine's "mistakes" are called to her attention by a countdown of dropped dinnerware: "Cordelia says, 'Think of ten stacks of plates. Those are your ten chances,' " and with each mistake Elaine makes a " 'Crash!' " leaves one stack less (171). This countdown calls to mind both *King Lear* and the Eaton's Catalogue. What "nothing" will be left when all the plates are dropped, and all the faults are added up? What then will be the nature of a poor, bare, forked, unaccommodated woman with nothing from the catalogues at all? It is rough play indeed that leads, with all that dropped imaginary dinnerware, to such elemental and tragic questions.

EXIT CORDELIA: PAIN'S PASSINGS

Elaine, like all of us, must carry with her the pains of her past. They are her heritage, much of what makes her who she is, and so it requires no retrospective with a concomitant return to Toronto to resurrect old suffering at the hands of Cordelia. For example, early in remembering (and recreating) her childhood she also recalls later times, the birth of her two daughters and how each time she would have preferred a son: "With sons [she] would have known what to do" (114). Her daughters, however, somehow knew what to do with her at even her worst times, "the days of nothing" when she "would lie on the floor in the dark, with the curtains drawn and the door closed" and try "to protect them" from even suspecting the existence of her despair by telling them that she had a headache or that she was working (114–15). "But they didn't seem to need that protection, they seemed to take everything in, look at it straight, accept everything. 'Mummy's in there lying on the floor. She'll be fine tomorrow,' I heard Sarah tell Anne when one was ten and the other was four. And so I was fine. Such faith, like the faith in sunrise or the phases of the moon, sustained me" (115). The reader is sustained too, for this passage operates as a synecdoche, presaging the passing of much of the pain inflicted by Cordelia, which will soon culminate in what one commentator, Anita Brookner, sees as almost — except for the youth of the perpetrator — "a clear case of attempted murder" (32).

Elaine's liberation from the tyranny of Cordelia is anticipated in other ways as well. After the torment at the hands of her friend during her second year in Toronto, Elaine and her family again adjourn to the north woods. But she does not revert to her old relationship with her brother, participating on his terms in what he wants to do (at this point playing chess and collecting butterflies). She is "ceasing to be interested in games [she] can't win" (144). This disinclination, like much else in the novel, contradicts her regularly asserted claim that boys are her allies, that she understands boys because they are direct and forward, and that all her problems are with girls. Just as her brother's play anticipated Cordelia's, her escape from his play anticipates her escape from Cordelia's. Why play at all, she is learning to ask herself, when to play is to lose.

This question, with respect to Cordelia, is soon posed more explicitly in the novel but before Elaine is ready to confront it. " 'You don't have to play with them,' [her] mother says. 'There must be other little girls you can play with instead.' " But when her mother goes on to tell Elaine " 'to learn to stand up for [her]self,' " to not be " 'spineless,' " and to not " 'let them push [her] around' " (156), that advice, valid as it is on one level, can seem to the daughter to be little more than playing the very game she is here being told not to play. It is still more testimony to her many faults and more evidence that she is being rightly punished because of those faults. At this moment, the most backbone Elaine can muster is to go on baking muffins with her mother (a hint of Elaine being similarly consumable, a junior version of the "edible woman"). She has, however, begun to practice covertly what her mother here counsels, and she continues to do so. She had earlier taken "to be[ing] sick more often" (137) and staying home from school and Cordelia. At those times she would work on her scrapbook and be the cutter, not the cut (another escape from the role of victim). She also discovers how to effect a similar evasion at school. Going with her father to a science display in his biology building, she faints when she sees the still-beating heart of a dead and dissected turtle and realizes that "[t]here's a way out of places you want to leave, but can't. Fainting is like stepping sideways, out of your own body, out of time or into another time. When you wake up it's later. Time has gone on without you" (171). She soon learns to leave the times of her "punishments" behind by fainting almost at will, a version of both relativity and dissociation. Elaine, in effect, enacts the speeding spaceship scenario her brother described earlier whereby "you could . . . exist in two places at once" (3). Indeed, Elaine's first faint is described in terms of a "rushing away" (170), and her subsequent ones leave her seemingly "looking down like a bird" (or a passenger in a spaceship) at what is transpiring below (172). Elaine above viewing an unconscious Elaine below gives us, of course, two Elaines as a graphic version of Atwood's characteristic figure, the self-divided female. Furthermore, the two Elaines we here encounter, "one superimposed on the other, but imperfectly" and with "an edge of transparency" (173), recall Elaine's opening image of time (and thus memory) as a series of overlaid transparencies. They also embody what might be termed the "two-Elaines" structure of the novel, with Elaine as both the present narrator and the protagonist whose past is being recounted. What Elaine observes of one episode of fainting in her past — "I'm not there. I'm off to the side" (173) — can just as validly apply to her whole telling of that past.

The mother's failure with her advice as well as Elaine's fainting both anticipate a more successful rescue, the "miracle" whereby through the appearance of the Virgin Mary Elaine is saved from what well could have been a death by freezing. This episode is one of the most important in the novel and so merits consideration at some length. To start with, the rescue both devolves from and delimits Cordelia's persecution of Elaine, which has grown "harsher [and] more relentless . . . as if she's driven by the urge to see how far she can go" and is "backing [Elaine] towards an edge, like the edge of a cliff" (154).

This figurative cliff, as a figurative culmination of the girls' relationship, suggests the ravine, and soon does so even more explicitly when Elaine contemplates suicide either by eating nightshade, drinking Javex, or "jumping off the bridge" and "smashing down . . . like a [Hallowe'en] pumpkin" (155). The escape offered by suicide is all the more tempting in that she imagines Cordelia advocating it, "not in her scornful voice" but "in her kind one" (155). The contradiction of a friend kindly telling you to kill yourself is further emphasized by Elaine hearing "bursts of laughter" as her parents play bridge. Confused by the name of the game, she feels that such festivity and fun "is not like a bridge" (158), certainly not like the bridge towards which she is being pushed.

Other events suggest the bridge as a metaphoric crossing to adult female sexuality. Particularly suggestive are a number of almost successive episodes. Elaine first notes that her three girl friends are pleased with the valentines they received from boys at the school party and can secretly exult in knowing that she received the most. Then, after commenting on ten-year-old Carol's developing breasts, she tells how Carol, spanked by her father on her "bare bum" for experimenting with lipstick (164), pulls down her pants at school the next day to show the red marks still present, that second red marking as sexual as was the first. Next, Carol wants the others to see the wet spot she found on the sheet of her mother's twin bed, but, since the bed has been made, the best they can do is look in the drawer of the bedside table where they find "a rubber thing like the top of a mushroom, and a tube of toothpaste that isn't toothpaste" (164). The mark of the lipstick reimposed as the mark of the spanking conjoins oral and anal sexual contact, and that toothpaste that isn't toothpaste similarly merges oral and genital. The girls then play doctor; to check Carol's heart Elaine has to feel her bare breast which "feels like a balloon [a condom?] half filled with water, or like lukewarm oatmeal porridge" (165). These two similes suggesting a prophylactic and a meal again conjoin the genital and the oral. This sequence of sexually suggestive actions concludes when Elaine's mother, one night, has a spontaneous abortion early in her pregnancy and is taken to the hospital. The wet spot Elaine didn't see on Carol's mother's sheet can now be seen as "a huge oval splotch of blood" on the mattress of her own parents' bed, and when her mother comes home from the hospital it's "as if she's gone off somewhere else, leaving [Elaine] behind" (166), which is partly a version of Elaine's own previous fainting.

Sex as improperly applied lipstick or improperly applied spankings? Sex as covertly playing doctor or as the real ambulance and being rushed to the hospital in the night? Sex for procreation or with birth control and only for pleasure? Sex as occasioning a birth or an abortion, a new life or a death? Sex as becoming an adult female who can be a mother herself or as losing one's mother while still a child? Not surprisingly, Elaine is confused, and her confusion is doubly expressed in denial and dreams. She maintains that her mother could not have been pregnant as her brother claims, for "women who are going to have babies have big fat stomachs, and [her] mother didn't have one." But she dreams "that [her] mother has had a baby, one of a set of twins," and that she doesn't "know where the other twin is" (166). She also dreams that her "parents are dead but also alive. . . . sinking down through the earth, which is hard but transparent, like ice" and "look[ing] up at [her] sorrowfully as they recede" (167). The "burial" of the parents in ground like ice looks back to Elaine's burial in the hole as a version of the ravine and forward to her falling through the ice in the ravine and her own brush with death as the sexual tensions of early adolescence implicit in these dreams and in the events that preceded them are partly played out on the bridge.

The episode on the bridge begins with more ominously suggestive play. It is March and, with winter ending, Cordelia takes off her mittens to throw snowballs, then throws herself on the ground to make a snow angel. "Where her hands stopped, down near her sides, are the imprints of her fingers, like little claws" (185) — a devilish angel in the dirty snow. Cordelia then falls again and slides down an icy hill, but not intentionally as Elaine originally thought, so Elaine must be punished for laughing at the mishap of her friend. Cordelia takes Elaine's hat, throws it off the bridge into the ravine, and tells her she will be forgiven if she goes down to retrieve it, all of which is done, not like the meting out of a real punishment, but "like someone giving instructions for a game" (187).

One obvious aspect of the "game" is its implicit sexuality. To start with, the ravine is where "bad men" supposedly hang out and where, consequently, good girls should never go, and all four of them have been explicitly warned against ever going there alone. Furthermore, Elaine's descent into the ravine partly reenacts Cordelia's previous fall to make that distinctly devilish angel in snow no longer white, and, like Cordelia's, Elaine's "fall" is also suggestively sexual. Elaine's hat is blue, the colour associated with the Virgin, so it is almost as if her virginity has been thrown away before she "falls" following it. It might also be noted that to throw away a girl's hat is to leave a maiden's head exposed, and much that same sexual point is also suggested by the fairy-tale implications of the scene. This entire episode could well be entitled "Blue Cap," a version — or inversion — of "Red Cap," which, as Wilson has argued at length, is a fairy tale that Atwood has used before as a fable of female sexuality, especially in *The Handmaid's Tale.* Just how and how much "Red Cap," like its analogue, "Little Red Riding Hood," encodes female sexuality has been studied by such scholars as Bruno Bettelheim, Ruth Bottigheimer, Jack Zipes, and the various contributors to Alan Dundes's *Little Red Riding Hood: A Casebook.* The throwing of the hat is also a symbolic castration or, perhaps more accurately, clitoridectomy. Something is taken from her as sign and summary of her quintessential lack, and, indeed, down in the ravine, Elaine agrees that "Cordelia is right," that "it's a stupid hat," and that she doesn't "want to wear it ever again" (187). Finally, the fall is a sexual sacrifice and a sexual scapegoating in that Elaine's forced descent into the ravine is intended to undo and reverse Cordelia's preceding fall down the hill, just as all of Elaine's supposed faults are projections — and thus also denials — of Cordelia's.

The blue hat, however, is also a version of Elaine's talismanic blue cat's eye marble, which introduces another range of intratextual references. For example, she had earlier dreamed that her "blue cat's eye [shone] in the sky like the sun" and then fell "down out of the sky, straight towards [her] head, brilliant and glassy," to strike her and pass into her "without hurting, except that it's cold," and the "cold wakes [her] up" (145). As a version of the falling hat, the marble is also suggestive of the ice onto which the hat falls, and when Elaine ventures out on the frozen stream to retrieve her hat, she goes through the ice just as the icy marble earlier went through her. "Cold shoots through [her]," and slabs of broken ice like "blue arches, blue caves, pure and silent" (like cold blue marble) surround her. She struggles out of the stream but, cold and exhausted, does not think she can climb out of the ravine and hears in the falling snow the "whispering" of "the dead people, coming up invisible out of the water" — which, as earlier noted, ran through the cemetery — to counsel rest (188). She records how she almost succumbs: "I know I should get up and walk home, but it seems easier to stay here, in the snow, with the little pellets of ice caressing my face gently. Also I'm very sleepy, I close my eyes" (189). The sleep she is here slipping into, as any good Canadian versed in winter survival (or who has read *Survival*) knows, is itself a bridge, an easy crossing from life to death by freezing.

It is at this point that the Virgin appears, first standing on the bridge and then floating down to enfold Elaine in a sense of happiness and warmth and to tell her silently that she *"can go home now,"* that *"[i]t will be all right"* (189). This figure accompanies Elaine and keeps her from feeling any cold or pain as she climbs up out of the ravine and makes her way along the streets until she meets her mother running towards her, looking for her. Then, when Elaine's mother throws her arms around her daughter, the other Mother is "suddenly gone," and Elaine feels "[p]ain and cold shoot back into [her]" (190). But now she is in no danger and is soon in bed with extra blankets and a hot water bottle where she dreams a version of what has just happened and what is yet to come. While running from a "lot of [shouting] people" who are chasing her, she is seized by an invisible hand and lifted up above them where she can no longer hear them (191). As with the fainting, but much more permanently, she will rise above what has previously tormented her. And when she returns to school, she has finally achieved immunity from Cordelia. At the first criticism she turns and walks away. "It's like stepping off a cliff, believing the air will hold you up. And it does. I see that I don't have to do what she says, and, worse and better, I've never had to do what she says. I can do what I like." She also recognizes the "game" for the game it always was. Cordelia's condemnations and commands are "an imitation," an "acting," an "impersonation, of someone much older" — of, to be more explicit, a disappointed parent (193). In short, Cordelia's need for the game is greater than Elaine's, for she must redeem her faults and failings by making them Elaine's, a passing on of pain and blame explicitly enacted on the bridge.

Elaine simply won't play that game anymore. This whole section of the novel portraying the pain inflicted on her by Cordelia and, she now realizes, by herself as well, ends with her recording the way her life at this point takes a new direction.

At school I make friends with a different girl, whose name is Jill. She is interested in other kinds of games, games of paper and wood. We go to her house and play Old Maid, Snap, Pick Up Sticks. Grace and Cordelia and Carol hang around the edges of my life, enticing, jeering, growing paler and paler every day, less and less substantial. I hardly hear them any more because I hardly listen. (194)

There are several significant reversals here. The childish games she plays with her new friend allow Elaine to retreat from the sexuality that led up to the episode on the bridge. Old Maid, the one game with adult implications, suggests a female sexuality quite different from that represented by Cordelia's and Elaine's "falls." The combination of Elaine and Jill, as opposed to Jack and Jill, is a Mother Goose alteration that counters the sexual implications of the "Blue Cap" episode as well as the original Mother Goose rhyme. There are no immediate prospects of more symbolic head injuries or tumblings down (Mother Goose rhymes can encode sexuality as much as fairy tales). Finally, as Grace, Carol, and especially Cordelia grow "paler and paler" and "less and less substantial," they become the ghosts that Elaine earlier impersonated in her Hallowe'en costume and enact her previous attempts at playing dead. By reclaiming her life, she has seemingly consigned them to a version of the living death they earlier tried to inflict on her.

I say "seemingly" because the ontological status of this episode is far from clear. As Sonia Gernes points out: "Atwood structures the events leading up to Elaine's vision so that the reader can . . . explain the vision in simple psychological terms. Elaine has both the need for a powerful female icon, and available images with which to construct it." Elaine, moreover, "is already off-balance and having out-of-body experiences" (148). She could well have imagined the Virgin, whose picture she had recently found and to whom she had fervently prayed. Elaine, too, views her "vision" as both real and fantasized. When she first describes the encounter with the Virgin, she insists on the actuality of this unlikely experience: "I know who it is that I've seen. It's the Virgin Mary, there can be no doubt. Even when I was praying I wasn't sure she was real, but now I know she is" (190). Near the end of the novel, however, she is equally insistent on its unreality:

There was no voice. No one came walking on air down from the bridge, there was no lady in a dark cloak bending over me. Although she has come back to me now in absolute clarity, acute in every detail, the outline of her hooded shape against the lights from the bridge, the red of her heart from within the cloak, I know this didn't happen. There was only darkness and silence. Nobody and nothing. (418)

But immediately after this insistence on "nobody and nothing," Cordelia makes her one appearance in the present time of the novel. It is a ghostly appearance, a ghost of the Cordelia of the past: "She's wearing her grey snowsuit jacket but the hood is back, her head is bare. She has the same green wool kneesocks, sloppily down around her ankles, the brown school brogues scuffed at the toes, one lace broken and knotted, the yellowish-brown hair with the bangs falling into her eyes, the eyes grey-green" (419). There are also ghostly hints of the Elaine of the past: "It's cold, colder. I can hear the rustle of the sleet, the water moving under the ice." There is another crucial recognition about the game they both played:

I know she's looking at me, the lopsided mouth smiling a little, the face closed and defiant. There is the same shame, the sick feeling in my body, the same knowledge of my own wrongness, awkwardness, weakness; the same wish to be loved; the same loneliness; the same fear. But these are not my own emotions any more. They are Cordelia's; as they always were. (419)

The present and the past, the different dimensions of time and space and memory, interconnect:

I am the older one now, I'm the stronger. If she stays here any longer she will freeze to death; she will be left behind, in the wrong time. It's almost too late.

I reach out my arms to her, bend down, hands open to show I have no weapon. *It's all right*, I say to her. *You can go home now.* (419)

Elaine, who has just insisted that nothing happened, here herself becomes the Lady of Perpetual Help, that "nobody" who wasn't there, and says to Cordelia — now the one in danger of freezing — precisely what the Virgin Mary earlier said to her. The Virgin Mary, like Cordelia, clearly still has "a tendency to exist" (242). Furthermore, the ghostly presence of Cordelia at the end of section seven is read differently when set against her even more ghostly presence at the end of the novel. More simply put, that first fading is not the whole story, for soon Cordelia reappears to play Elaine to Elaine's Cordelia. The pain does not end, and Elaine finds herself passing back to Cordelia the same suffering that Cordelia first passed on to her.

* * *

Section eight, "Half a Face," following the chapter that describes the intercession of the Virgin, begins with two oddly juxtaposed episodes. Elaine first remembers how "[f]or a long time, [she] would go into churches" thinking she wanted "to see the art" but actually "looking for" a statue of the Virgin Mary that represented the entity she had encountered in the ravine (197). Eventually, in an old church in Mexico and on her first trip with Ben, who will become her second husband, she finds an image of the figure who appeared to her, "the only one of [many] wood or marble or plaster Virgins who had ever seemed at all real to [her]" (198). The statue, covered with small pinned-on images of prayed-for items, is "a Virgin of lost things." What, Elaine asks, is lost so that she can pray for it or pin a picture of it on the statue? She partly answers this question after Ben finds her lying on the floor in the church. In answer to his question if she is " 'all right,' " she says she's "forgotten how [she] got down there" (198). Time is lost and so is she.

The second episode is her recollection of the death of the King the fall following the appearance of the Virgin and Elaine's subsequent emancipation from Cordelia's rule. *The King is dead,"* she thinks (200). "Now all the things that happened when he was alive are over and done with: the war, the planes with only one wing, the mud outside our house, a lot of things." That last indefinite "a lot" speaks volumes about what she wants to forget. Soon she is insisting that not only has she "forgotten things" but that she has "forgotten that [she has] forgotten them" (200). The claim itself is a contradiction that is further contradicted when Elaine immediately goes on to list many of these forgotten items: stacks of plates, the fainting, not liking Mrs. Smeath, the ravine, the appearance of the Virgin. There are also grounds for doubting the self-proclaimed happiness that supposedly follows from all of this forgetting and that is supposedly proved by her Grade Six class picture in which she is broadly smiling and, in her mother's expression, *"[h]appy as a clam."* "[H]appy as a clam," she repeats, with a significant addition, "hard-shelled, firmly closed." That hard-shelled quality of her asserted happiness is seen even in the prose of this section of the novel. In flat, declarative, affectless sentences, she claims to have no feelings at all. Thus, of the names of her three former friends, she can assert: "There is no emotion attached to these names. They're like the names of distant cousins, people who live far away, people I hardly know" (201). Whatever they might have done to her is reduced to "something like a sentence in tiny dry print on a page, flattened out, like the dates of ancient battles." With her own immediate past recast as distant and generic "history," again, as even Elaine acknowledges, "[t]ime is missing" (201), and much of Elaine is missing too.

The King is dead but the Queen is not. Elaine notes that she now has a new school not on the far side of the ravine, so there is no longer any need to cross the old bridge over the ravine to go to the old Queen Mary School. That name serves to connect the two opening episodes of this chapter, for the wife of the dead king and the Virgin are both named Mary and one was Queen of England and one is Queen of Heaven. Moreover, Queen Mary of England has now become Queen Mother Mary, another conjoining of the two Queens. With this linking, metaphors of mothering, of caring and helping, converge with metaphors of empire, of conquering and ruling, and that merging is particularly suggested by the third Queen Mary who has been named in the novel, Mary, Queen of Scots. Elizabeth is now Queen, but an earlier Queen Elizabeth ordered the execution of the Scottish Queen Mary. So the "ancient battles" that Elaine would like to use to distance herself from her own history are not, like the one between these two Queens, really all that distant, and not just because Elaine played Queen Mary in the burial game. The history of England's defeat of Scotland is itself replayed in two contexts in *Cat's Eye*: in the juxtaposition of two teachers in Queen Mary School, and in Elaine's move from a school named for the English Queen Mary (not the Scottish one) to the rigorously Scottish Burnham High School. Old battles and the kings and queens of England and Scotland are deeply embedded in this text, and not just through the presence of *Macbeth* as an intertext.

Miss Lumley, the first teacher Elaine encounters who "rules by fear" and delights in administering the strap (78), is a proponent of English rule and the British Empire:

> "The sun never sets on the British Empire," says Miss Lumley, tapping the roll-down map with her long wooden pointer. In countries that are not the British Empire, they cut out children's tongues, especially those of boys. Before the British Empire there were no railroads or postal services in India, and Africa was full of tribal warfare, with spears, and had no proper clothing. The Indians in Canada did not have the wheel or telephones, and ate the hearts of their enemies in the heathenish belief that it would give them courage. The British Empire changed all that. It brought in electric lights. (79)

She is succeeded by Miss Stuart with her Scotch burr and her gentler ways and her picture of Bonnie Prince Charlie, whose last name, Elaine notes, is also the teacher's. Old battles are given still another contemporary reference when Miss Stuart becomes a proponent of home rule, so to speak, and allows Elaine to paint her picture as she sees it rather than as others might prefer it to be seen. For Miss Stuart, the harrowing of Elaine might well be a version of the harrowing of Scotland, and there is lots of room for black rather than "all [those] pink parts of the map" that Miss Lumley proudly pointed to when claiming that British rule had weaned dark peoples from their evil ways and lifted them up from benighted savagery into the light of civilization.

The novel does have clear postcolonial implications. Miss Lumley advocates the conventional ordering of an imperial centre and subsidiary margins which necessarily fall short of that centre even as they are ostensibly being re-created in its image, all of which Elaine slyly (albeit unintentionally) critiques in her own appropriately imperfect reproduction of her teacher's teaching. "Because we're Britons," Elaine muses one morning after the class has sung "God Save the King" and "Rule Britannia," "we will never be slaves. But we aren't real Britons, because we are also Canadians. This isn't quite as good, although it has its own song ["The Maple Leaf Forever"]" (80). Miss Lumley's imagined navy-blue bloomers are, as one section title asserts, "Empire Bloomers," and in imperialistic terms too Elaine can be afraid that they might signify that something is wrong with her. She is, after all, both female and Canadian.

The position Elaine occupies with respect to Cordelia and the other three girls — on the margin and not quite measuring up — has obvious colonial (and thus also racial and religious) analogues in the text. She is, for example, early struck by how much the plight of Mr. Banerji, her father's student from India, parallels her own. Similarly, she is attracted to Mrs. Finestein, for whom she works briefly as a baby-sitter, because this Jewish woman can happily ignore prevailing Christian conceptions of what a wife and a mother should be. Moreover, Christian concepts of how things should be justify missionary work and the converting of "heathens" or the punishing of them for persisting in their evil ways. Elaine, named a "heathen" by Mrs. Smeath and her missionary sister, bitterly resents this designation and all it implies. Further considerations of who rules and to what end are raised throughout the novel. Carol Osborne, for example, points out how Elaine's resistance to Cordelia is "associated with blackness," while Cordelia and her cohorts are "aligned with white images" (104). The usual symbolism of white and black is thereby reversed, and Elaine "aligns herself with minorities, both literally and figuratively, in order to overcome the oppression of white, middle-class Canadian society" (105). This oppression, of course, mirrors still others, such as Canada's subjection to both British and American imperialism.

Indeed, Burnham High School, with its official school plaid, thistle crest, and Gaelic motto, and with a picture of Dame Flora MacLeod, the head of the MacLeod clan, hanging next to the portrait of the Queen, reproduces in a Scottish register the very claims of ascendancy that it disputes in their more standard English version. The students are even "encouraged to think of [Dame Flora's] castle as [their] ancestral home, and of Dame Flora as [their] spiritual leader." They "learn 'The Skye Boat Song,' about Bonnie Prince Charlie escaping the genocidal English." Elaine thinks "all this Scottishness is normal for high schools, never having gone to one before," and notes that she, along with even "the several Armenians, Greeks, and Chinese [is Dame Flora really their spiritual leader?] in [the] school lose the edges of their differences, immersed as [they] all are in a mist of plaid" (206).

This "mist of plaid" suggests *Macbeth*, which, with its Birnam woods, conversely suggests the name of the school. *Macbeth*, in fact, even comes to Burnham school when a visiting theatre company performs the play at the high school. Cordelia assists in the performance and is most pleased, as Elaine "can tell" by how she "acts bored and nonchalant," to be part of the world of real theatre, real pretence (244). She passes on to Elaine actors' jokes and snippets of stage lore, like how "real actors will never say the name *Macbeth* out loud, because it's bad luck" and call the play " 'The Tartans' " instead (245). Elaine points out that Cordelia has just said " 'Macbeth,' " and bad luck enters right on cue. Handling the props, Cordelia replaces the cabbage that was to play the cut-off head of Macbeth with a fresh one which, thrown down at the conclusion of the performance, bounces "right across the stage like a rubber ball, and falls off the edge," turning the resolution of the tragedy into a laughable farce. A "mortified" Cordelia later laments that she didn't know that it "was *supposed* to be rotten," but she gets no sympathy from Elaine, who seizes the opportunity to tease her friend unmercifully (245).

The second round of Elaine and Cordelia's friendship has from the first been premised on their inequality and on Elaine this time having the upper hand. It begins when Cordelia's mother calls Elaine's mother the day before Elaine starts high school to see if Elaine will walk to school with Cordelia and, in effect, sponsor her in the new school which will be just as new to Elaine. They will also be in the same classes. Elaine has skipped a grade; Cordelia, who earlier skipped a grade, has now failed one and has also been expelled from her last school. Elaine succeeds academically in high school; Cordelia does not. She also does better socially. Her "mean mouth" wins her friends and status, and the person she uses it "on the most is Cordelia." As Elaine observes, "She doesn't even have to provoke me, I use her as target practice" (235). Elaine is comfortable with boys, while Cordelia is always striking the wrong note and saying the wrong thing. When they double date — ventures arranged by Elaine — Cordelia's date is always the less desirable one. Elaine as a teenager gets along reasonably well with her brother, her mother, and her father, while Cordelia does not measure up to her stylish older sisters and continues to disappoint her parents, particularly her "wolvish" and "ponderous" father, whom Elaine can manage, striking the right, light "give and take" note that seems to be "what he wants" from the women in his life: "But Cordelia can never come up with it, because she's too frightened of him. She's frightened of not pleasing him. And yet he is not pleased. I've seen it many times, her dithering, fumble-footed efforts to appease him. But nothing she can do or say will ever be enough, because she is somehow the wrong person" (249).

Elaine does not place the blame for Cordelia's failings where it obviously belongs, on the father who sees "nothing" in his third daughter because she is not the son he would have preferred. Here again we can see that Atwood as author does not necessarily subscribe to Elaine's habit of letting men off the hook. Elaine, of course, has her own unacknowledged reasons for blaming Cordelia for any present suffering, which are suggested by her angry reaction to Cordelia's interaction with her father: "It makes me want to kick her [Cordelia]. How can she be so abject? When will she learn?" (249). Those last two questions have been heard before in the novel.

There are other echoes from their childhood past in the teenage "friendship" of Cordelia and Elaine. Elaine generally chooses not to hear them, as when Cordelia throws herself down to make a snow angel one day and for "some reason [Elaine doesn't] like the sight of her lying there in the snow, arms spread out," and insists that she get up (229). Similarly, Elaine and Cordelia now consign the absent Grace Smeath to the role of misfit, a role Elaine formerly filled, and mock Grace and her family as the "Lump-lumps," the appropriate subjects of savage jokes: " 'What does the Lump-lump Family have for dinner? Plates of gristle!' "; " 'What does Grace Lump-lump do for fun? Pops her pimples!' " (230). Elaine finds all of this "a deeply satisfying game" but "can't account for [her] own savagery" in playing it (231), just as she later asks "how [she] can be so mean to [her] best friend" when she mocks Cordelia for the cabbage fiasco (246). She plays other versions of past games as well, and does not see their origin either. For example, Elaine repeats Cordelia's earlier scare tactics and engages in her own "death games" at Cordelia's expense. Stopping one evening in the same cemetery through which the stream of the "dissolved" dead flows, Elaine claims that she is not really alive, that she is a vampire who can seemingly go about in the daylight only because she also has a non-vampire twin who passes as Elaine while the real Elaine, the vampire Elaine, is safely asleep in her earth-filled coffin. Cordelia's reluctance to enter this game only prompts Elaine to carry the play further with the dubious reassurance that her companion has nothing to fear.

> I lower my voice. "I'm just telling you the truth. You're my friend, I thought it was time you knew. I'm really dead. I've been dead for years."
>
> "You can stop playing that," says Cordelia sharply. I'm surprised at how much pleasure this gives me, to know she's so uneasy, to know I have this much power over her.
>
> "Playing what?" I say. "I'm not playing. But *you* don't have to worry. I won't suck any of your blood. You're my friend." (233)

There are another two Elaines here besides the two Elaine posits. One is playfully teasing Cordelia. The other is not playing; she *has* been dead for years; she will suck her friend's blood because her friend sucked hers. Twinned twin Elaines also reflect Elaine and Cordelia as doubled versions of one another, each tormentor and victim of the other.

One obvious intertext for this torment is *Macbeth*. As Douglas Glover observes, Elaine's three childhood friends are, from the start, a version of the three witches in Shakespeare's play, and, as already noted, both Cordelia and Elaine play Duncan to the other's Macbeth and Macbeth to the other's Duncan. This intertext is itself then doubled and inverted with the two horror comics that Cordelia in a minor rebellion at one point pinches. True trash mirrors tragedy, and both mirror Cordelia and Elaine. Thus the first comic-book story they read is "about two sisters, a pretty one and [an ugly] one who has a burn covering half her face" (211). The ugly one commits suicide in front of a mirror and then through the mirror somehow takes over her sister's body and lives her life, now ugly only in her mirror reflection, until the beautiful one's boyfriend recognizes, in the mirror, what has happened and shatters the mirror. Mirror play, grotesque deformations, false identities, revenge, and returns from the dead run through these tales, as in another horror story "about a dead man coming back out of a swamp, covered with dripping, peeling-off flesh, to strangle the brother who pushed him into the swamp in the first place" (212). This is the return of the repressed with a vengeance, and another version, like *Macbeth*, of Elaine's return to extract vengeance which will later, with Elaine's attempted suicide, be reenacted as Cordelia's return to the same end.

The extent to which Elaine and Cordelia mirror one another is made explicit late in their high-school friendship and serves as a basis for the termination of their relationship. One day Cordelia recalls the holes she used to dig behind her house (holes Elaine claims to have forgotten) and muses how she wanted to put a chair in one and be by herself safely out of the way. " 'Safe from what?' " Elaine inquires:

"Just safe," she says. "When I was really little, I guess I used to get into trouble a lot, with Daddy. When he would lose his temper. You never knew when he was going to do it. 'Wipe that smirk off your face,' he would say. I used to stand up to him." She squashes out her cigarette, which has been smouldering in the ashtray. "You know, I hated moving to that house. I hated the kids at Queen Mary's, and those boring things like skipping. I didn't really have any good friends there, except for you." (252)

Programmatic forgetfulness cannot quite protect Elaine from a distorted version of her past that reflects what she is doing in the present. She has a sudden brief glimpse of Cordelia as a nine year old and with that glimpse comes a rush of shame and nausea:

A wave of blood goes up to my head, my stomach shrinks together, as if something dangerous has just missed hitting me. It's as if I've been caught stealing, or telling a lie; or as if I've heard other people talking about me, saying bad things about me, behind my back. There's the same flush of shame, of guilt and terror, and of cold disgust with myself. But I don't know where these feelings have come from, what I've done. (253)

Nor does she want to know. They had been telling chicken jokes. Elaine immediately tells another one: " 'Why did the unwashed chicken cross the road twice?' " The answer, " 'Because it was a dirty double-crosser' " (253), is her unconscious admission of her betrayal of Cordelia, of Cordelia's earlier betrayal of her. It is also, with a chicken joke now doing much the same intertextual work as *Macbeth*, another suggestion of the pervasiveness of doubling and crossing in the novel. Indeed, Elaine doubly double-crosses Cordelia, first by mistreating her and then by dropping her. She soon "begin[s] to avoid Cordelia" (254), and their second exercise in being friends is, for all practical purposes, over.

Some time later, however, she paints Cordelia, and much of their past is evoked in this portrait. The painting is one of three reproduced in a newspaper article on the retrospective show. Reading the article, Elaine contemplates "the only picture [she] ever did of Cordelia. . . . *Half a Face*, it's called: an odd title, because Cordelia's entire face is visible. But behind her, hanging on the wall, like emblems in the Renaissance, or those heads of animals, moose or bear, you used to find in northern bars, is another face, covered with a white cloth. The effect is of a theatrical mask. Perhaps" (227). The title, to the reader and at this point, is not so odd. Cordelia's face is also Elaine's, and so is only half Cordelia's. This point is not masked by the theatrical effect of "another face, covered with a white cloth." As "theatrical" implies, this is the cabbage head of Macbeth, the murderer murdered, and so it is also both Cordelia and Elaine. As a title, *Half a Face* also looks back to the horror comic book and the ugly sister with her half-burned face who possessed the beautiful sister, which again points to Cordelia and Elaine as both victim and victimizer. Elaine remembers that she wanted to paint Cordelia at "about thirteen, looking out with that defiant, almost belligerent stare of hers. *So?*" Yet she had "trouble with this picture," with "fix[ing] Cordelia in one time, at one age," and particularly with "the eyes" which "sabotaged" her and looked "[f]rightened" rather than "strong," making Cordelia's face appear "tentative, hesitant, reproachful." But Cordelia's belligerent stare was always a theatrical mask for her doubts and fears, just as Elaine's mean mouth wasn't the whole story either and was also a compensation and a cover-up. "Cordelia is afraid of me, in this picture," Elaine sees in the narrative present, and she, moreover, is "afraid of Cordelia," not "of seeing Cordelia," but "of being Cordelia. Because in some way [they have] changed places, and [Elaine has] forgotten when" (227).

Yet the resonance of the role each has long played in the other's life can hardly be reduced to a single reversal in the past. Even in the painting they are still changing places (which "half" of which head — the fully revealed or the fully covered one — is Elaine's and which is Cordelia's?). Furthermore, Elaine has just read the covert attack, veiled by faint praise, that a young woman journalist (a version of Cordelia) wrote for the local paper. Staying at the studio of her artist ex-husband, who now does special blood and gore effects (cabbages wrapped in tea towels no longer serve) for horror movies that are themselves versions of both Shakespearean tragedies and of the horror comics Elaine and Cordelia earlier read, Elaine thinks she "should be deliberately provocative" by going to the opening wearing "some of Jon's axe-murder special effects, the burnt face with its one peeled bloodshot eye" (226). The "half-a-face" look Elaine here contemplates pairs with her *Half a Face* painting of Cordelia, even as the half-defaced face she envisions also confirms her own suspicion that all she has done to Cordelia, as a version of what Cordelia did to her, she has also done to herself as a version of Cordelia.

THE PORTRAIT OF THE YOUNG
ARTIST AS A FALLING WOMAN

The difference between what Elaine shows in her painting of Cordelia and what she says in her comments on that painting (describing it only on a most obvious surface level) is a measure of one motive behind her choice of vocation. Part of art's appeal is that she can reframe through her paintings aspects of her life and issues from her past that she might not otherwise be able to address. Yet Elaine tries to disguise even this indirect form of dealing with her past. As she later notes about another significantly titled painting, *Falling Women*, "[a] lot of [her] paintings . . . began in [her] confusion about words" (268). But her subsequent description of this painting that is ostensibly really "about men" — even though there are no men in it — attests that there are more underlying confusions than the colloquial problem of deducing just what the *fall* of a fallen woman entailed. Elaine goes on to explain that the missing men of "the kind who caused women to fall" are actually present in the painting as "a line of sharp slippery rocks with jagged edges" through which one "could walk with care . . . and if you slipped you'd fall and cut yourself, but it was no use blaming the rocks." For Elaine, "That must be what was meant by fallen women. Fallen women were women who had fallen onto men and hurt themselves." The painting itself portrays not two but three such women on their way to being hurt:

Fallen women were not pulled-down women or pushed women, merely fallen. Of course there was Eve and the Fall; but there was nothing about falling in that story, which was only about eating, like most children's stories.

Falling Women showed the women, three of them, falling as if by accident off a bridge, their skirts opened into bells by the wind, their hair streaming upwards. Down they fell, onto the men who were lying unseen, jagged and dark and without volition, far below. (268)

Elaine herself is definitely one of these women, even though, in portraying her childhood "fall" from the bridge, she tries to turn it into something else, just as she also tries to turn the biblical account of Eve's fall into something else, a children's story about eating. Another one of the three women in the painting is Cordelia, who is both a double of Elaine and who, at this point in the novel, has also fallen, at least into the mental breakdown for which she was institutionalized and perhaps into suicide as well. The third, I would suggest, is Susie, whose affair with their art teacher preceded Elaine's. So Elaine and Susie are doubles too. The painting comes closer to home than Elaine admits, and presents a somewhat different story than the one Elaine recounts in remembering it. But that is not necessarily the whole story either, for one purpose of the present and past narratives in *Cat's Eye* is to tell the larger story of the paintings, a story not always told *in* the paintings. Witness, for example, those rocks, stand-ins for men who are thereby absolved of volition and responsibility in all dramas of female falls, innocent as the weather: "They merely drenched you or struck you like lightning and moved on, mindless as blizzards" (268). Cordelia's father hardly validates this view, nor does Elaine's art teacher, nor does her first husband whom she meets at art school.

From the beginning, art, for Elaine, allows both confrontation and evasion. Thus the collage of her childhood scrapbook participates in the game of the symbolic construction of the perfect woman even as it also critiques it (particularly with those cut-off heads and headless bodies that go into making various versions of the perfect woman). Similarly, her first described picture, one done in Miss Stuart's class, captures her sense of the bleakness of her life at this time while also showing her safe from what is making her so wretched. Miss Stuart asks the class to portray what they do after school. Even then Elaine wants to draw with a difference and not produce the "skipping ropes," the "jolly snowmen," the "playing with a dog" she knows her classmates will render. She decides to show herself in bed at night, and after drawing the room and the bed with her in it, she starts to "colour in the night" (162). As she does so, her "hand holding the black crayon presses down, harder and harder, until the picture is almost entirely black, until only a faint shadow of [her] bed and [her] head on the pillow remains to be seen." Elaine in bed at home and thus not playing with Cordelia is also Elaine as the "nothing" to which that play is reducing her. The double focus of the painting is then reproduced in the two different reactions of pupil and teacher. Elaine is dismayed that she has done "the wrong thing" and that Miss Stuart will be "disappointed in [her]." The teacher, however, merely asks why the drawing is " 'so darruk, my dear' " and then responds, " 'I see,' " to Elaine's "idiotic answer" that " 'it's night,' " while touching her gently, reassuringly, on the shoulder (162). With her blue eyes, blue like Elaine's cat's eye marble, Miss Stuart can also see in the dark, into the darkness of the drawing and the drawer.

Miss Stuart's concerned touch and teaching are obviously in contrast to the touch and teaching that Elaine later encounters in another art class. While taking her final high-school examinations and in the middle of a biology test in which she knows she will do very well because she "can draw anything: the insides of crayfish ears, the human eye, frogs' genitalia, the blossom of the snapdragon," and "in cross section" too, Elaine has a conversion experience that "comes to [her], like a sudden epileptic fit" and realizes that she's "going to be a painter," not a biologist (255). To that end, she enrols in an Art and Archaeology program at the University of Toronto (the closest she can get to art at that institution) and in a night class on life drawing at the Toronto College of Art. For the second course she needs the consent of the instructor. When she shows him her first fumbling attempts at oil painting along with some of her more professional high-school biology drawings, he decides to accept her largely on the basis of how little she has done: " 'You are a complete amateur,' he said. 'But sometimes this is better. We can begin from nothing. . . . We will see what we can make of you' " (271–72). Elaine is again reduced to "nothing," and the question of what might be made out of this nothing recalls Cordelia's pre-adolescent program of remaking

Elaine, the game that reduced her to nothing in the first place. " 'You are an unfinished voman,' " Mr. Hrbik, the art teacher and a refugee from Hungary, is soon saying, " 'but here you will be finished' " (273). There seems to be no finishing to the finishing of Elaine. But she scores a small triumph in her first encounter with her future teacher, a triumph she can recognize only in retrospect. One of the biology drawings she shows him is of " 'the reproductive system of a . . . male frog' " (271), which has a certain relevance with respect to both Mr. Hrbik's name and intentions.

Elaine's life-drawing class recalls two of her childhood classes as well as her schooling at the hands of Cordelia. Looking at "the first live naked woman [she has] ever seen, apart from [herself] in the mirror" (269), she is frightened by the model's stocky body, with its squashed out buttocks, flabby stomach, and saggy breasts, because that is what she herself might turn into, just as she was earlier afraid of Miss Lumley's adult sexuality. Once she merely imagined Miss Lumley with her bloomers off; now she actually sees such a figure, and must draw it too. Of her first drawings, her teacher critically observes, " 'We are not making a medical textbook. . . . What you have made is a corpse, not a woman' " (272). But he tempers that criticism by telling her to save what she has done so that she can later see how far she has come. Then, like Miss Stuart, he gives her arm an encouraging squeeze.

Mr. Hrbik's intentions, however, are different from Miss Stuart's. Elaine's grade-school play with Cordelia was, as noted, partly a pre-adolescent experimenting with sex. Her post-high-school foray into art soon devolves into a late-adolescent experimenting with sex as well. Mr. Hrbik's project of "finishing her as a voman" entails her seduction as well as her training in art techniques. When it comes to young attractive women, the two programs, for this teacher, are inextricably intertwined. When Elaine first enters the class, he is having an affair with the young, blonde, and buxom Susie, but not with either of the two older women, Marjorie and Babs, who are professional artists in a minor way and are taking the course as a refresher. And why, one could well ask, are young women required to pay extra, sexually, for their education, whereas the young men who constitute most of the class can simply be taught whatever knowledge Mr. Hrbik has to impart to them? This is a question that never occurs to Elaine, who has a penchant for accepting uncritically the working of the very double standard that is working against her. For example, Elaine notes of Susie, "I think of her as a silly girl who's just fooling around at art school, too dumb to get into university, although I don't make judgments like this about the boys" (282). There are other judgements she doesn't make about "the boys" as well. Their derisive dismissal of " 'lady painters' " (279) and crude sexist comments — " 'Cunt like an elephant's arse' " — about the female models' attractions (the models' availability being taken for granted) roll right off Elaine, who doesn't "resent any of this" but thinks she is "privileged . . . an exception, to some rule [she hasn't] even identified" (280).

Elaine is no more perceptive in other areas. She misses the obvious clues that Susie and Mr. Hrbik are having an affair and then, when this fact is brought home to her, mistakenly decides that "it's Mr. Hrbik who loves Susie," that Susie is "too shallow" to be in love and is only "toying with him" (285). She also casts Susie as a "[h]ard as nails" femme fatale, "straight out of forties movie posters," and thus "in control," while Mr. Hrbik supposedly "staggers besotted towards his fate" (285). All of this construction is, of course, fantasy and wish fulfilment, as Elaine presently discovers when her own affair with Mr. Hrbik turns out to be rather different from her Hollywood-inspired imaginings of what such "romance" should be.

The novel's framing of Elaine's seduction suggests that she, like Susie, will have no grand passionate relationship. To start with, the whole account of the beginning of the affair is preceded by Elaine's memory of the beginning of its end. She recalls going with Josef to Toronto's only French restaurant at that time, La Chaumière, which wasn't the " 'thatched cottage' " its name promised, "but a prosaic, dowdy building like other Toronto buildings" (292). The French meal wasn't really French either. Josef observes that the snails aren't fresh but canned, and Elaine, in turn, notices that he "says this sadly, with resignation, as if it means the end, though the end of what is not clear." She notes, too, that "this is how he says many things" and "was the way he first said [her] name, for instance" (292). Elaine then recalls reviewing in the restaurant the course of their affair, after which she eats "another tinned, inauthentic snail" and realizes "with no warning that [she is] miserable" (299). Between one snail and another falls the shadow of the end, and that shadow is the fact that the affair has been, from the beginning, as dubious as

Josef's self-proclaimed European sophistication, as inauthentic as the restaurant and its snails.

The beginning of the relationship was not particularly promising either. At the conclusion of the life-drawing class, and while standing in line with Babs and Marjorie waiting for her termination interview as a student (which, it turns out, will also be her hiring interview as a mistress), Elaine hears Marjorie tell Babs about an encounter with a flasher in Union Station. " 'Can't you do any better than that?' " Marjorie had asked. As the two older women joke " 'about wee-nies' " and " '[n]o wonder the poor boob runs around in train stations trying to get somebody to look at it' " and " 'what goes up must come down' " (292), Susie comes crying out of Mr. Hrbik's office. Younger and less experienced than Marjorie, Elaine will not — at least at first — laugh at the "poor boob's" shortcomings when Mr. Hrbik's courting turns out to be only slightly more polished than the flasher's.

Her teacher's cursory evaluation of her progress in his course soon devolves to his sad repeating of her name. He takes her hand and then, still sitting at his desk, draws her down to kneel "between his knees" where he both caresses and kisses her (293). She notes that she had "never been kissed that way before" and that it "was like a perfume ad: foreign and dangerous and potentially degrading" (293–94). She can either "get up and run for it" or remain "for one more minute" and so move forever beyond "groping[s]" in movie theatres and automobiles and "skirmishes over brassiere hooks. No non-sense, no fooling around" (294). The obvious foolishness of her anticipated affair, its theatricality, and the degree to which it too will soon be an undoing of buttons and bra hooks, all suggest how much Elaine is fooling herself in her claim that she will leave fooling around behind her by allowing herself to be seduced.

As noted, she is "miserable" in the affair. One source of her unhappiness is the consideration that she has not replaced Susie in Josef's life but has, instead, merely been added to her. All is quite comfortable for Josef, however. He can maintain that Elaine is everything to him and have his Susie too. Small wonder that Elaine presently decides that what is good for the gander might be good for the goose as well and supplements Josef with another man (signifi-cantly, one of her high-school papers was on polyandry). Spending the summer in Toronto to be available for Josef and waitressing in a depressing fast-food restaurant, she encounters Jon, who had also taken the life-drawing class, and goes out for a drink with him after work. She intends a return to her former camaraderie with the male students in the art class, but the evening ends on a different note. When she starts crying as they leave the beer parlour, he comforts her — " 'Hey, pal,' he says, patting [her] awkwardly. 'What's wrong?' " — which only makes her "cry even more" (307). He then takes her to his apartment: "There are no lights on. I put my arms around his waist and hold on as if I'm sinking into mud, and he lifts me up like that and carries me through the dark room . . . and we fall together onto the floor" (308). Making love on the floor is a descent, and into figurative mud at that. It is repetition (reenacting how she and Josef began their affair) as reversal (doing to Josef what he has done to her) as the same old story of doublings and betrayals and falls.

* * *

Elaine's affair with two men mirrors Josef's with two women, and she notices his dubious double standard threat when he casually claims, once his suspicions are aroused, that a man should have the right to kill his woman and her lover but "says nothing about what a woman does, in the case of another woman." She finds that deception agrees with her and adds drama to her life. "Two men are better than one," she decides, because she doesn't "have to make up [her] mind about either of them" (316). Josef balances her against Susie; she balances Josef against Jon; and Jon obviously has other women in his life and his bohemian walk-up apartment as well. But this elaborate dance of deception and overlaid intersecting affairs begins to collapse with Susie's abortion, and with that abortion we have another example of the deep patterning in the novel and of how Elaine both sees and doesn't see that design which is also the pattern of her life.

Before the abortion, Susie comes to the restaurant where Elaine works to ask Elaine if she knows where Josef might be found. Elaine lies that she doesn't and also notes how "plaintive" and "hopeless" Susie seems, how much she "was letting herself go" (319). This judgement has already been applied by Cordelia to Elaine, and by Elaine to Cordelia, so Susie is yet another version of the two of them. Moreover, when, sometime later, Susie calls Elaine with a desperate cry for help and Elaine goes to her apartment to find blood everywhere and Susie nearly dead from a botched abortion, Elaine sympathizes with Susie's plight but only partly. "[T]here is also another voice; a small, mean voice, ancient and smug, that comes from somewhere deep inside my head: *It serves her right*" (321). " 'It serves her right' " is precisely what Mrs. Smeath earlier said of Elaine's "punishment" at the hands of her three friends (180). So Susie as a victim as a version of both Elaine and Cordelia, prompts Elaine to become a version of Mrs. Smeath, someone who sanctions the suffering of others. Hilde Staels even suggests that Elaine has substantially become a Mrs. Smeath, "a cold . . . old woman who cannot forgive" and who thereby also "suffers from a diseased heart" (186).

The abortion entails minor echoes of the more immediate past as well. Elaine has just remembered how at Jon's disordered apartment she would regularly find, as part of "the morning remains of an all-night party, . . . someone tossing their cookies in the toilet. 'Tossing their cookies' is what Jon calls it. He thinks it's funny" (317). At Susie's she finds a different morning-after mess. Seeing all the blood, Elaine vomits into the blood-filled toilet; it isn't at all funny. When Elaine sees Susie "lying on the bed in her pink nylon shortie nightie, white as an uncooked chicken," the unlikely simile is more a measure of death and undoneness, of being consumable and expendable (like tossed cookies) than of Susie's actual flesh tone. Susie, Elaine also sees, is hardly a femme fatale; neither is she the abject victim of passion nor the pathetic product of its passing. "The pink nightie [especially] brings it home to [Elaine that Susie] is none of the things" Elaine has imagined and "never has been. She's just a nice girl playing dress-ups" (320). Much the same, of course, could be said of Elaine herself, for she is not quite playing the free-wheeling role she wants to think she is either.

The image of Susie as an uncooked chicken also brings in the matter of wings. In the immediate context, Elaine, seeing Susie on the bed, also sees that "[u]nderneath her, across the sheet, is a great splotch of fresh blood, spreading out like bright red wings to either side of her" (320). These wings of blood, as a version of bloody feet, are a sign of the limitations imposed on women and represent another example (albeit disguised) of Atwood's use of the "Red Shoes" fairy tale which she employed more obviously in earlier works such as *Lady Oracle* and *The Handmaid's Tale*. The wings relate, too, to the suggestions of women falling and women flying that run throughout the text. The account of the abortion, for example, comes in the section entitled "Falling Women," which is also the title of one of Elaine's paintings. Susie lying on the bed, a fallen virgin, is partly Elaine fallen into the stream (that stream of "death" itself repeated in the flowing blood that is also the sign of being female) and partly Elaine's mother who was taken to the hospital following a spontaneous abortion the sign of which was "a huge oval splotch of blood" on the bed (166). The wings of blood also recall other references to wings in the novel. "I am eating lost flight" (131), Elaine thinks of the turkey wing she is served one Thanksgiving dinner. At that same dinner, her father offers Mr. Banerji a slice of wing and observes, " 'You can't fly on one wing' " (129), which brings in another series of wing references starting with Stephen's favourite childhood song, "Coming in on a Wing and a Prayer," the World War II song about the airplane that made it safely back despite losing one engine. Stephen, however, later does not make it back from his last flight that is grounded by the hijackers. He is picked as the passenger who is to be killed to show that the hijackers are serious. Shot and thrown from the airplane onto the tarmac, he, too, exemplifies lost flight as he falls "faster than the speed of light" into death, into "the past" (391). Wings, as both Susie's abortion and Stephen's death attest, do not always carry one to safety, to where one wants to go.

There is still another sense in which Susie doubly sets the pattern for Elaine at this point in her life. First, after the abortion, Susie will have nothing more to do with Josef, and when the "full weight" of him and his melancholy mourning on how he has lost both Susie and his baby falls on Elaine, she decides to dump him too, an act she finds "enormously pleasing" (322). And then she also soon finds herself in Susie's condition, unmarried and pregnant and afraid to tell Jon, just as Susie was afraid to tell Josef: "I think about things I've heard: drinking a lot of gin, knitting needles, coat-hangers; but what do you do with them? I think about Susie and her wings of red blood. Whatever it was she did, I will not do it. I am too frightened. I refuse to end up like her" (336). Elaine, however, is more like Susie than she wants to admit. After the final break with Josef she dreams not of him but of Susie "in her black turtleneck and jeans" (Elaine's standard dress at the time as well), shorter and younger, with a pageboy haircut (Cordelia's childhood cut), "holding a coiled skipping rope, licking one half of an orange popsicle," and "spitefully" asking, " 'Don't you know what a twin set is?' " (323). As a child, Elaine's failings included not knowing about twin-set sweaters or twin beds. She is still having some problems with twin sets: Susie as Cordelia's twin; Cordelia as Elaine's; and Susie as Elaine's.

The thematic connection between Susie's "wings" and Stephen's points to still another twin set. As much as Elaine doesn't understand him or his work as a theoretical astrophysicist, Stephen is also her double, as is suggested even by the brief and loaded postcards he occasionally sends to his sister. "*Got married. Annette sends regards*" (330), he jots on the back of a San Francisco postcard showing the Golden Gate Bridge in the sunset. That sunset is not auspicious and neither is the city nor the bridge (considering his sister's previous experience with bridges). "*Got divorced,*" he writes several years later, this time with even more obvious irony, on the back of "a postcard of the Statue of Liberty" (330–31). Elaine can "assume he has been puzzled by both events," as if they "have happened to him accidentally, like stubbing your toe" or "walking . . . into a park, in a foreign country, at night, unaware of the possibilities for damage" (331). Her subsequent marriage and divorce, described in more detail than his, will also be a venture into a foreign realm replete with unrecognized or unacknowledged dangers, rocks over which she can trip. Her attempted suicide when her marriage begins to deteriorate is a partial reenactment of Susie's bloody botched abortion just as it is also a foreshadowing of Stephen's death, which is also anticipated by his own more minor misadventures, such as his attempt to collect butterflies on the military testing range.

Elaine's pregnancy, viewed from the first under the sign of Susie's wings of red blood, anticipates her attempted suicide. Much the same point is made by her reaction upon finding out she is pregnant: "I go back to my apartment, lie down on the floor," she remembers. "My body is numb, inert, without sensation. I can hardly move, I can hardly breathe. I feel as if I'm at the centre of nothingness, of a black square that is totally empty; that I'm exploding slowly outwards, into the cold burning void of space" (336). Cordelia's and Susie's (after the abortion) "nothing" is here magnified to Stephen's cosmic black hole level. But the cataclysm in Elaine's life is also described as business as usual. "One day, when nothing has changed, nothing has been done or happened that is any different from usual, I discover I am pregnant" (336). The adult female sexuality Elaine has long played at and feared — Miss Lumley's bloomers, the scrapbooks, the games with her friends — now fully confronts her. Part of what she contends with is the "nothing" of the quotidian (the way she and Jon are simply enacting society's usual pattern of people pairing off into heterosexual couples). The signs are not particularly promising here either. Just before she discovers she is pregnant Elaine describes how, at this time, the two of them are half-living together. "Jon stays over three or four nights a week," and she doesn't "ask what he does on the other nights," an arrangement which sounds suspiciously like the one Josef previously had with her. When Jon does stay over he acts like "he is making a large concession," as though this is something she wants, and, she admits, maybe it is (335). When he isn't there she leads much the same bohemian life that he does, but when he is there she will fix them both regular meals and do the laundry, his as well as hers:

> "You're the sort of girl who should get married," he says one day, when I appear with a pile of folded shirts and jeans. I think this may be an insult, but I'm not sure.
> "Do your own laundry then," I say.
> "Hey," he says, "don't be like that." (336)

He wants both his freshly washed clothes and the right to demean her for being so straight. So which woman is she supposed to be like, the one who does the laundry (and the dishes and the cooking) or the one who doesn't?

Her own deep ambivalence about domesticity is indicated by the way she begins, right after the pregnancy, to paint differently:

> Until now I've always painted things that were actually there, in front of me. Now I begin to paint things that aren't there.
> I paint a silver toaster, the old kind, with knobs and doors. One of the doors is partly open, revealing the red-hot grill within. . . .
> I paint a wringer washing machine. The washing machine is a squat cylinder of white enamel. The wringer itself is a disturbing fleshtone pink. (337)

She goes on to say that although "these things must be memories," they do not seem so to her but "are simply there, in isolation, as an object glimpsed on the street is there." Yet what she claims is without context in the present definitely has a context in the past. We remember how, as a child, she wanted to put her finger on the red-hot wires of the toaster as an escape, an alternative to the pain Cordelia inflicted; or how she wanted to put herself through the wringer (and considering her recent exchange with Jon about the laundry, the wringer obviously has a present context too). So when Elaine notes that although the pictures are "suffused with anxiety, . . . it's not [her] own anxiety" but an "anxiety [that] is in the things themselves" (337), this observation is no more accurate than her claim that there is no context for the paintings. Elaine has already remembered how, as a child, she used to help her mother with the wash in the "small and enclosed, secret, underground" laundry room, rather like a cellar or a grave. At the time, she noted the various "odd, power-filled substances" required, particularly the "Javex bleach with a skull and crossbones on it, reeking of sanitation and death" (122). As she fished garments that felt like "a drowned person" from the rinsing tub and fed them through "the two rubber rollers, the colour of pale flesh," she wanted, despite warnings that "women can get their hands caught in wringers," to put herself through (122).

> I think about what would happen to my hand if it did get caught: the blood and flesh squeezing up my arm like a travelling bulge, the hand coming out the other side flat as a glove, white as paper. This would hurt a lot at first, I know that. But there's something compelling about it. A whole person could go through the wringer and come out flat, neat, completed, like a flower pressed in a book. (122–23)

With the pregnancy, she is again being pressed into a role she doesn't want to play: the flat figure of the perfect lady — wife and mother — from the catalogue games of her girlhood. No wonder her paintings conflate domestic appliances and torture devices.

Jon and Elaine do get married. She is grateful that he didn't want her to have an abortion and pleased that he obviously loves their baby when she is born. But soon the marriage is going badly and they are having fights that are mostly about who gets to remain a child, who gets to go on "running away from the grownups" instead of becoming one (341). Jon usually wins these fights. He even uses their daughter as a way of marginalizing his wife and scoring small symbolic victories over her. " 'Let's hide on Mummy,' " he says, coming home, "scoop[ing] Sarah up . . . [and] putting the two of them into the same camp, in pretended league against" Elaine, which "annoys [her] more than it should" (340). Elaine does not want to recognize how this game partly repeats her painful past and still marks her as the excluded one even though she has now achieved the purported goal of the earlier game, the adoption of a standard version of domesticity.

Elaine's barely suppressed anger brings her to a women's discussion group, where again she half acknowledges and half denies the tensions in her life, both in the present and in the past. She can agree that "what is wrong with us [the women at the meeting] the way we are is men" and concur with the accusations made against men: that "[t]hey are violent"; that "[t]hey shove the housework off on women"; that "[t]hey are insensitive and refuse to confront their own emotions"; that they are sexually gullible and "with a few gasps and wheezes they can be conned into thinking they are sexual supermen" (344). But even as Elaine listens to the "giggles of recognition" prompted by this last charge, she also "begin[s] to wonder if [she's] been faking orgasm without knowing it" (344). For her, the rule of the "Phallus" still applies, even as women are laughing at the shortcomings of the penis and its claims to mastery. If there is any liberating "laughter of Medusa" (to borrow Hélène Cixous's title) in this scene, Elaine doesn't hear it. Instead, and predictably, the laughter seems to be directed at her.

The feminist "meetings are supposed to make [her] feel more powerful, and in some ways they do." She finds it "exciting," to hear what the other women have to say and can "begin to think that women [she has] thought were stupid, or wimps, may simply have been hiding things, as [she herself] was." Nevertheless, she continues, "these meetings also make [her] nervous, and [she doesn't] understand why" (344). When, however, she goes on to describe how she feels "awkward and uncertain," how she fears she will say or do "the wrong thing," and how she suspects that she has "no right to speak," as if she's "standing outside a closed door while . . . disapproving judgments are being pronounced, inside, about [her]" (344–45), the reader has no problem recognizing the source of these reactions. Sisterhood might be powerful in the present, but for Elaine it is more powerful in the past, and in her own version of the return of the repressed the women's group becomes a replay of how she painfully played as a girl at those games ostensibly designed to turn her into the perfect daughter of the patriarchy, precisely what the other members of the group are trying not to be. "Sisterhood is a difficult concept for me, I tell myself," Elaine maintains, "because I never had a sister. Brotherhood is not" (345). The self-deception of that conclusion is registered not just by the undercutting self-reflexivity of "I tell myself." Elaine insists that if men are the problem, that is just another problem women bring upon themselves and deserve for bringing it on — "If you stay with the man, whatever problems you are having are your own fault" (344) — even as she also maintains that men aren't a problem. Neither side of the contradiction, much less the contradiction itself, allows her any grounds for voicing any of the problems she had with Josef and is having with Jon, including such minor ones as the double bind about doing the laundry.

* * *

Elaine's ambivalence about feminism, obvious in her account of her participation in the women's group, also characterizes her subsequent participation, with three other women artists from this group, in her first show, an exhibition of art by "women only" (347). Again, Atwood presents this scene ironically, revealing to the reader more than Elaine is willing to see in her own narration of her first success. For example, Elaine notes the show's possible dangers: It "is risky business, and [they all] know it." But whereas Jody, one of the other artists, observes that they well might "get trashed, by the male art establishment" with its traditional male bias and its suspicion of women artists and even more so of feminist artists, Elaine's immediate worry is that they "could get trashed by women as well, for singling ourselves out, putting ourselves forward" (347). Old fears and contradictions still prevail — as if it is the business of women to be unobtrusively perfect while intrusively policing the perceived imperfections of other women.

Elaine's past is evoked both in her fears about the possible consequences of a successful show and in the art of the other women who exhibit with her. The show is held in what was formerly a small supermarket that still has "a few tattered signs" including "FRESH FROM CALIFORNIA. MEAT LIKE YOU LIKE IT" (349). Jody suggests that they " 'make this [unpromising] space work for [them].' " She " 'didn't take judo for nothing,' " and they can " '[l]et the momentum of the enemy carry him off balance.' " She thereupon proceeds to incorporate the MEAT LIKE YOU LIKE IT sign into one of her fashion mannequin constructions, "an especially violent dismemberment in which the mannequin, dressed only in ropes and leather straps, has ended up with her head tucked upside-down under her arm" (349). The defunct supermarket setting, the beheaded and bound mannequin, and the transposed sign all contribute to this construction's success as a critique of how women are socially constructed as constrained and self-divided mindless bodies that exist to serve the needs and pleasures of others. Jody's mannequin thus represents what Elaine has long been schooled to be — a consumable product, a being without voice or agency to be moulded into what others would make of her, into "meat like you like it." More specifically, the head tucked under the mannequin's arm also brings to mind *Macbeth*, death, and cabbage heads, and so underscores how dubiously both Elaine and Cordelia have played the deadly roles assigned to them.

The work of one of the other women artists is relevant as well. Zillah produces what she calls *Lintscapes* out of the fluff taken from clothes-dryer filters. These recall Elaine's childhood interest in the detritus of consumerism and how she was especially fascinated with silver cigarette paper, which she collected and wanted to turn into art (one of her pieces in this show is a construction entitled *Silver Paper*). Zillah's *Lintscapes* also reflect Elaine's long involvement with laundry, from helping her mother as a child — with the attendant temptation to flatten herself — to the more recent question of to do or not to do Jon's (and *Wringer* is another piece Elaine has in the show). However, the main point here is the difference between the genesis of *Lintscapes* and *Wringer*. Zillah buys various towels and puts "them repeatedly through the dryer, to get [the] shades of pink, of grey-green, of off-white" (348) that she requires for her cloud-like constructions. She is doing laundry for her own reasons, for the sake of her art, and not for someone else's reasons, to be made (flattened or fluffed) into the kind of woman he both wants and doesn't want.

Not surprisingly, Elaine soon feels that the work of the other women artists (that there are three of them significantly recalls her three childhood friends) is better than her own and thus a measure of how she, with her "too decorative" and "merely pretty" paintings, has "strayed off course" and "failed to make a statement" (350). At the opening, too, she notices that the other artists "all seem to have more friends than [she does], more close women friends" (351). This lack is an "absence" she claims she's "never really considered . . . before." But if she still sees other women as the measure and proof of her failures as a woman, it is hardly surprising she finds it hard to have many female friends or that she is reluctant to inquire closely why. And when she goes on to reassure herself that "[t]here is, Cordelia, of course," this foregrounding of someone she admits she hasn't "seen . . . for years" only emphasizes her lack of women friends and that her real problem is not quite her problem as she sees it. Equally dubiously, she surveys the room to see if Jon has arrived yet (he had promised to come to the opening) or, failing that, if there is "someone inappropriate" with whom she might "flirt . . . just to see what could happen; but there aren't many possibilities, because there aren't many men" (351). Even at the feminist art show, Elaine believes she can be validated as a woman only through a man's desire, however transient and meaningless that desire might be. As an artist, Elaine and, even more so, Atwood both know better.

At this point Elaine is singled out to be trashed and by another woman at that, not by a man. A number of Elaine's paintings of Mrs. Smeath, together entitled *White Gift*, portray that hated woman in various stages of undress and exposure that also mock her pretensions to Christianity. In one of these, "THE • KINGDOM • OF • GOD • IS • WITHIN • YOU," Mrs. Smeath is portrayed "in her saggy-legged cotton underpants, her one large breast sectioned to show her heart" as "the heart of a dying turtle: reptilian, dark red, diseased" (352). The attack on Elaine's art comes from a woman who might be "another Mrs. Smeath . . . stepped down off the wall" with "the same round raw-potato face" and "hulky big-boned frame." This person, whom Elaine first thinks is Grace Smeath now grown into a version of her mother, "stalks, rigid and quivering" with rage towards the painting (352). She tells Elaine that she is " 'disgusting' " for " 'taking the Lord's name in vain' " and " 'want[ing] to hurt people' " and that she " 'ought to be ashamed of [her]self' " (353). The woman then hurls an open bottle of ink onto one of the paintings, "veiling Mrs. Smeath in Parker's Washable Blue," whereupon she gives Elaine "a triumphant smile" and scurries from the room (353–54).

Being verbally attacked, Elaine finds, is no longer as painful as it was in the past. The derogatory terms are much the same as those formerly directed against her by her childhood friends. Now, however, it is the other woman who is going too far. So Elaine can be both "aghast" and "deeply satisfied"; someone else "is making a spectacle of herself, at last, and [Elaine is] in control" (353). After the attack, Elaine is "soothed and consoled" by the other women, as if "maybe they like [her] after all" (354). Furthermore, the attack itself is reassuring: "paintings that can get bottles of ink thrown at them, that can inspire such outraged violence, such uproar and display, must have an odd revolutionary power" (354). This is reminiscent of Elaine's later reaction (even though it comes earlier in the novel) when she sees a defaced poster for the retrospective exhibit and is pleased with the result. The moustache looks good on her. She has "achieved, finally, a face . . . that attracts moustaches. A public face, a face worth defacing. This is an accomplishment." Instead of demonstrating that you are nothing, an attack can testify that you "have made something of [your]self, something or other, after all" (20).

"FEATHERS FLY AT FEMINIST FRACAS," reports the local newspaper about the opening, and Elaine registers the "comic" and demeaning intent underlying this report of "henfighting." The article also delivers the anticipated attack on women's art, deploying the predictable "bad adjectives: 'abrasive,' 'aggressive' and 'shrill' " (354). In *Wilderness Tips*, Atwood will subsequently mock the anti-feminist intent of such gendered words by having the narrator of "Weight" and her friend, Molly, come up with their own definitions, such as *shrill*, "a sharp-beaked shorebird," or *strident*, "a brand of medicated toothpick" (181), or *menopause*, "a pause while you reconsider men" (185). In *Cat's Eye*, however, Atwood simply shows how these pejorative adjectives can be used, judo style, to make the enemy's momentum — and vocabulary — work against him. One of the artists, Carolyn, "makes a bright yellow banner with the words 'abrasive,' 'aggressive' and 'shrill' on it in red, and hangs it outside the door" (354). Attendance goes up dramatically.

Elaine's first art show also brings about her final meeting with Cordelia, who reads the newspaper account and calls Elaine from the mental hospital where she has been confined following a suicide attempt. Elaine visits her, takes her out to a corner café, much like the ones they frequented as teenagers, and hears Cordelia's plea for help. " 'Elaine,' she says, 'get me out,' " even as Elaine recognizes that in some seemingly irretrievable way Cordelia has let herself go or, more accurately, has "let go of her idea of herself" and is "lost" in some place where Elaine "can't get at her" (358). Cordelia, however, can still get at Elaine, who, when asked to help, "seeth[es] with a fury [she] can neither explain nor express" (359). Elaine turns Cordelia down, consciously noting the objections Jon might raise and the dangers Sarah might be subjected to, as well as her own sense of "not feeling totally glued together [her]self" at the time (359) — an assessment that recalls Jody's "sawn apart" and "glued back together" mannequins (347).

Elaine and Cordelia are still both divided and connected. " 'So you won't,' [Cordelia] says. And then, forlornly: 'I guess you've always hated me' " (359). This second statement elicits Elaine's "shocked" denial. Cordelia, as Elaine recently claimed at the show, is her one friend. They are also, individually and jointly, divided from and connected with their joint pasts. Elaine's refusal prompts Cordelia's assertion that she will save herself: " 'I'll get out anyway,' she says. Her voice is not thick now, or hesitant. She has that stubborn, defiant look, the one [Elaine] remember[s] from years ago. *So?*" (359). The old Cordelia is not totally lost, and her idea of herself is still in there someplace, even if Elaine at first can't see it. Neither can Elaine see the old Elaine still present inside herself. "I can't remember ever hating Cordelia," she claims, but in the upsurge of unexamined rage at Cordelia's plea for help, Elaine wants to "rub her face in the snow," which clearly evokes the snowscape scene when Cordelia abandoned Elaine in the cold and thus partly explains Elaine's refusal to help as well as her anger at being requested to do so.

Much the same point is made when Elaine subsequently dreams of "Cordelia falling, from a cliff or bridge, against a background of twilight, her arms outspread, her skirt open like a bell, making a snow angel in the empty air" (360). This snow angel recalls Cordelia's earlier fall in the snow, which became the basis for Elaine's twilight fall under the bridge and into the frozen stream. Furthermore, Elaine awakes from these dreams with her "heart pounding and gravity cut from under [her], as in an elevator plummeting out of control" (360), falling herself in her dream of another's fall. She also dreams of one of Jody's mannequins, "hacked apart and glued back together," dressed only in a costume of spangled gauze and carrying, "[u]nderneath its arm, wrapped in a white cloth, . . . Cordelia's head" (360). The not-completely-glued-together mannequin is a version of Elaine as "not . . . totally glued together" just as it is also a version of Cordelia mad or playing mad. In her last encounter with Cordelia, Elaine reminds herself that her friend is "an actress" who "can counterfeit anything" (358). The wrapped head in the dream recalls, in the theatre register, Cordelia's *Macbeth* fiasco with the cabbage, just as the mannequin's costume evokes Cordelia's success as an attendant spirit in *The Tempest*. Elaine, however, while viewing that performance, could not recognize Cordelia beneath her spangled gauze costume. She is still having problems seeing through costumes and roles; nor can she understand, much less transcend, such questions as why she and Cordelia still play each other and why neither can help the other when the play goes badly.

The climax of Elaine and Cordelia's mutual doublings comes with the growing crisis in Elaine's marriage. She and Jon are fighting more and more, and she is "begin[ning] to see how the line is crossed, between histrionics and murder" (346). He is involved with other women and is not hiding this state of affairs. Elaine has found hairpins she knows are not hers in their bed. One night he does not come home. No longer having time or energy to paint, despite having just won a small government arts grant, Elaine is exhausted, dispirited, left in the cold (it is winter) by her husband to sit in the dark and contemplate the "ruin [she has] made" (373). She decides that whatever "is happening to [her] is [her] own fault," that she is "inadequate and stupid" and "might as well be dead" (372). Acting on this decision with her husband's Exacto knife, Elaine is also following Cordelia's example and command, for she hears a "voice, not inside [her] head at all but in the room, clearly [telling her]: *Do it. Come on. Do it.* This voice doesn't offer a choice; it has the force of an order. It's the difference between jumping and being pushed" (373). It is also the "voice of a nine-year-old child," neither "frightening" nor "menacing but excited, as if proposing an escapade, a prank, a treat" (374).

The voice, of course, is Cordelia's, and it is prompting Elaine to an act obviously more suicidal than was her descent into the ravine and out onto the ice to retrieve, also at Cordelia's orders, her hat. In both cases, too, the "difference between jumping and being pushed" collapses when one is pushed into jumping, when external judgements become so internalized that one consents to one's asserted nothingness and to the action that can easily follow from that estimation of worthlessness. Moreover, just as Elaine had turned the game of improvement back onto Cordelia and tormented her for not measuring up, Cordelia may now be turning the tables back on Elaine. The turning point, for Elaine, came when Cordelia sent her down into the ravine and left her there. Elaine has recently and rather similarly abandoned Cordelia by refusing to help her escape from the asylum. As Elaine subsequently notes, Cordelia "knows [Elaine has] deserted her, and she is angry." After a letter to Cordelia at the asylum comes back marked *"address unknown,"* Elaine realizes that Cordelia "could be anywhere" (360). Furthermore, Stephen once observed, when discoursing on matter as mostly empty space, energy, and probability, that " 'Cordelia has a tendency to exist' " (242). So Elaine's contradictory claim about Cordelia's voice — "I know it wasn't really there. Also I know I heard it" (374) — is doubly justified. First, a Cordelia with "a tendency to exist" and who "could be anywhere" blurs presence and absence. She is always a kind of resonance structure and uncertainty principle, and that is how she will continue to operate in Elaine's life and memories. Second, her wavering existence fits the pattern of the novel's mirror-play structure. The ontological uncertainty about Cordelia as the agent who sends Elaine a second time to a near death reflects the ontological status of the Virgin as the agent who saved Elaine the first time — she was also both there and not there. Furthermore, Cordelia, by prompting Elaine to attempt suicide, is also a version of the Virgin who earlier saved her. After almost committing suicide, Elaine knows if she remains in Toronto she "will die," that the city, "as much as Jon," is "killing" her (375). She soon leaves Toronto to live in Vancouver, taking Sarah with her. Cordelia, in effect, gets Elaine away from the city and out of her disastrous marriage, even though Elaine did not get Cordelia out of the asylum — yet another of those inverted reflections that characterize their ongoing relationship. Elaine's fall into attempted suicide, like her fall through the ice beneath the bridge, results in her being figuratively lifted out of a disastrous relationship and into a new life.

The figurative lift is in fact only to a somewhat different life because Elaine continues to be haunted by her past. In Vancouver, and starting over as a mother and artist, she will still sometimes lie crying on the floor at night, "washed by nothing" and thinking of how easily at this last Pacific "edge, of the land" she "could get pushed over" (377). Both the nothing she feels and the push she fears are obvious legacies of Cordelia. She also evinces the same ambivalence to feminism that she felt "back east," noting, for example, how lesbianism, as a model for a possibly equal relationship, would be impossible for her:

> I am ashamed of my own reluctance, my lack of desire; but the truth is that I would be terrified to get into bed with a woman. Women collect grievances, hold grudges and change shape. They pass hard, legitimate judgments, unlike the purblind guesses of men, fogged with romanticism and ignorance and bias and wish. Women know too much, they can neither be deceived nor trusted. I can understand why men are afraid of them, as they are frequently accused of being. (378–79)

But this distinction between women's "legitimate judgments" and men's "purblind guesses" is itself undone by Elaine's own self-deceptions. She still views herself as fundamentally flawed — "hopelessly heterosexual, a mother, quisling and secret wimp," someone with both a "blotchy and treacherous" heart and shaved legs. This judgement is neither legitimate nor her own; it is a legacy from her past with Cordelia. It is not Cordelia's judgement either, but her transmission of her father's judgement of her. Thus Elaine's sense that she is "nothing" ultimately derives not from a woman's "legitimate" assessment but from a man's biased wish. Elaine also admits that feminist women make her "nervous" because they "want to improve" her. This unfair assessment of feminism as merely an adult version of the childhood game of criticism, itself a version of the adult game of trying to produce the perfect patriarchal woman, is the precise opposite of what feminism seeks to accomplish. And when Elaine then records the anger that feminist discourse, as she

89

sees it, elicits in her — "*Bitch*, I think silently. *Don't boss me around*" (379) — she sounds remarkably like a terminally sexist man, which is yet another undercutting of her distinction between women and men, between the truths of the former and the errors of the latter.

She can "envy" her feminist associates "their conviction, their optimism, their carelessness, their fearlessness about men, their camaraderie," but she seeks for herself different "women friends, not very close ones," who are single mothers with whom she can "trade kids for nights out and grumble harmlessly" — as opposed to critiquing seriously. This is, she recognizes, "an older pattern, for women," and resembles the relationship of Babs and Marjorie in the drawing class, but she is "now . . . older" too (379). She also remarries, and in an older mode as well. Ben soon does her taxes, and her books, and her kitchen spices, arranging them alphabetically on a shelf he also built. He is a man right out of "the women's magazines of long ago," she recognizes when, early in their relationship, he comes over with his own saw and hammer to fix her back porch and then has "a beer afterwards, on the lawn, as in ads" (381). He is "also like an apple, after a prolonged and gluttonous binge," and she likes the easy comfort he offers as well as the pleasure he takes in her, in tending to her.

Elaine's account of her contented second marriage with Ben might seem to be belied by her prior telling of how, back in Toronto, she spends one final night with Jon. The point of this episode, however, is not what it reveals about her relationship with her present husband, but how it shows her beginning to come to terms with the more distant past of her first affair, her first marriage, and particularly the breakup of that marriage. During the day preceding her last night with Jon, Elaine walks past what was once Josef's house but is now apparently an antique shop. She has just eaten at a retro fifties diner where they had everything right except the price. A lot of the past, it seems, is being recycled. On seeing his house, she recalls that Josef had done some recycling too. He finally did make his movie, an art film about two "nebulous" women in gauzy dresses who did crazy things because they were both in love with the man in the film who loved both of them (364). One, blonde, obviously based on Susie, "took apart a radio . . . , ate a butterfly, and cut the throat of a cat" (365). The other, dark, modeled on Elaine, slashed her thighs with a razor and "jumped off a railway overpass, into a river" (this last action suggests that Elaine had told him about the bridge and the icy stream in the ravine). She also notes that the two women are virtually indistinguishable (except for their hair), but that this equivalence is the product of Josef's misunderstanding: "[I]t wouldn't have occurred to him that they might have had reasons of their own for being crazy," reasons that didn't derive from men. In short, Elaine and Susie were no more "real to Josef" than he was to Elaine. She admits that she "was unfair to him" but that such unfairness was essential: "Young women need unfairness, it's one of their few defences. They need their callousness, they need their ignorance. They walk in the dark, along the edges of high cliffs, humming to themselves, thinking themselves invulnerable" (365).

She immediately acknowledges that just as Josef constructed his preferred vision of her, she has constructed her image of him — and of Jon — in one of her paintings. *Life Drawing* depicts a partly draped naked woman whose head is a sphere of blue glass, and who is being painted by both Josef and Jon, themselves portrayed stark naked but "somewhat idealized" (365). Josef's rendering is a voluptuous woman with a Pre-Raphaelite face; Jon's "is a series of intestinal swirls, in hot pink, raspberry-ripple red and Burgundy Cherry purple" (366). There is considerable recycling here too and on different levels. Burgundy Cherry, for example, was the one flavour of ice cream served in the fast-food chicken restaurant where Elaine worked the summer of her affair with Josef and where Jon encountered her to begin their affair and subsequent marriage. Josef's Pre-Raphaelite rendering is the woman he wanted Elaine to be, and what he dressed her as, to take her to dinner at the Park Plaza Hotel Roof Garden. Jon's swirls represent the art style he practised at the time of his first involvement with Elaine, even as, with their lipstick and ice-cream flavour colours, they also hint at the lifestyle he then practised, sampling different women almost on a flavour-of-the-day basis. More obviously, the model's head derives from Elaine's blue cat's eye marble as well as from her early painterly fascination with reflective surfaces, the woman's head here reflecting to each man his own idea of how a woman should be rendered. As McCombs has noted, Elaine's painting, by portraying the portraying of the con-structed woman, reverses even as it reproduces "life drawing" (15). The usual gender and working of the gaze is inverted. We see not the naked woman as seen by a man, but the naked men not seeing a woman, and it is the men who are here revealed, right down to the "wonderful bums" Elaine recalls they both had (366).

The conflation of Josef and Jon in the painting is then followed by a different conflation in the narrative present. Right after describing *Life Drawing*, Elaine agrees to go out with Jon for drinks. At her suggestion, they go to the roof bar of the Park Plaza Hotel, which was formerly the restaurant to which Josef took her on their first "date." Afterwards, she and Jon take a taxi to his studio, just as she and Josef took a taxi to Josef's place (which she has also just visited). Jon's hand is on her waist as they ascend the stairs, repeating Josef's gesture on a similar occasion, a touch that both claimed her as his and at the same time attempted, as did all of his caresses, to press her (wring her, iron her, shades of laundry past) into the woman he would have preferred her to be. In Jon's studio, they make love on a mattress on the floor, as she earlier did for the first time with Josef on his floor and, for that matter, with Jon too the first time in his apartment.

This episode in the narrative present is not portrayed as a farcical attempt by an aging pair to reenact what didn't play particularly well with their first performance. Instead, it is one of the most tender scenes recorded in the novel. In Elaine's words:

> We undress each other, as we used to do at first; but more shyly. I don't want to be awkward. I'm glad it's dusk; I'm nervous about the backs of my thighs, the wrinkling above my knees, the soft fold across my stomach, not fatness exactly but a pleat. The hair on his chest is grey, a shock. I avoid looking at the small beer-belly that's grown on him, though I'm aware of it, of the changes in his body, as he must be of mine. (367)

Particulary suggestive here is Elaine's registering the differences between their present and past bodies and recognizing the physical facts of aging flesh — her pleated stomach, his beer belly — as compared to the constructed (whether idealized or demonized) versions of self and other that she needed in the past. With the loss of youth, or perhaps with the gain of having that youth safely in the past, a different innocence is achieved. Thus this love-making can signify back into time and redefine who and what they were rather than misleading both of them with promises of the future they were both avid for and with images of who and what they might become. Elaine notes that there is "comfort" in seeing that she can still "recognize" Jon, that she "could recognize him in total darkness" (cat's eyes again). That recognition is also a farewell. "It's the last look, before turning away, at some once-visited, once-extravagant place you know you won't go back to. An evening view, of Niagara Falls" (368). Niagara Falls was where they didn't go for the "joke" honeymoon that Jon suggested but that Elaine refused because "[w]hatever else we were getting into as the weeks passed ... and my body swelled like a slow flesh balloon, it was not a joke" (340–41). Now, with her body altering in a different fashion, she can get the earlier joke. It is in this sense that she can claim that she is not being "disloyal to Ben" but is merely settling an "old score" that long "pre-dates him" and really "has nothing to do with him" (368). She is putting a different finish to her past relationship with Jon: "The former anger is gone, and with it that edgy, jealous lust we used to have for each other. What's left is fondness, and regret. A diminuendo" (368). Her view of the fundamental innocence of the affair is further validated by the way the scene ends with Elaine kissing Jon "again, on the cheek this time" and noticing how his hair "is already turning white," whereupon she concludes, "we did that just in time. It was almost too late" (368). The head partly covered by white hair hints, like the cut-off head covered by a white cloth, that plays — with their role reversals and reenactments — eventually come to an end, and that she and Jon are running out of time.

This episode is one of the key retrospectives in the novel in that the past is revisited rather than merely recorded and is revisited to be redeemed rather than to be reversed. Reversal generally leads to more of the same, not to resolution. By merely switching roles as victim and victimizer, Elaine and Cordelia do not alter the rules of the game, and neither one is likely to free the other from the consequences of still playing the same game. Similarly, Josef's pain is no more real to Elaine than hers is to him, so the two can hardly look to one another for sympathy, much less for alleviation from suffering. This playing with pain is tracked back in the novel to Elaine's childhood war games with her brother. But in contradistinction to Stephen's directive, "Lie down, you're dead," she, aging herself, can finally, in effect, say to an obviously aging Jon: "Let's lie down together one last time, for we are still alive."

Elaine's recollection of her unhappy marriage with Jon, her flight to the West Coast, and her second marriage comes between her account of the final night with Jon and of that night's aftermath. The next morning Elaine looks back on what seems both a "dismissal" and a "blessing" for the two of them, like a mediaeval painting of a saint with a "hand raised, open to show there is no weapon: *Go in peace*" (385). She is, however, not yet ready to go in peace back to Vancouver, and neither does she want to oversee the hanging of her paintings. Instead of going to the gallery to see that the exhibit is in order, she takes the subway to the cemetery she and Cordelia used to walk past. The focus on the past, on the dead (her brother), and on the possibly dead (Cordelia) is further emphasized by her noting the occasional jack-o'-lantern and realizing it is All Soul's Eve "when the spirits of the dead will come back to the living, dressed as ballerinas and Coke bottles and spacemen and Mickey Mice, and the living will give them candy to keep them from turning vicious" (387). She also contrasts the Mexican festival of the dead with the Canadian one. The Mexicans have graveyard family picnics, with food for the living and candles for the dead, whereas Canadians have "rejected that easy flow between dimensions: we want the dead unmentionable, we refuse to name them, we refuse to feed them. Our dead as a result are thinner, greyer, harder to hear, and hungrier" (387).

The first hungry ghost Elaine acknowledges is her brother Stephen. The full account of his death on a hijacked airplane comes at this point in Elaine's narration and is itself an account replete with its own ghostly echoes. Sandwiches of cheese and dubious meat spread, for example, were served on the hijacked plane, so Stephen's "hands smell[ed] of old picnics, the roadside lunches of wartime" (389), a reference to his and Elaine's childhood past during World War II. The hijackers, with pillowcases over their heads, suggest to Elaine the "characters in old comic books [which Stephen collected], the ones with two identities" (390). She doesn't note two other possibilities from her past: the hijackers as children in Hallowe'en costumes or decapitated heads (like Macbeth's) shrouded in white cloth. When Stephen is the passenger selected to be executed, Elaine hopes that he was pushed from the plane before he was shot "so he could have had that brief moment of escape, of sunlight, of pretended flight" (392). But regardless of which action came first, Stephen doesn't come in on a wing and a prayer. He dies, instead, of the war broken up yet still going on, of the play of war turned real, of too much justice, of lost flight.

94

Stephen's death presages the death of Elaine's parents. They never recovered from his demise and after it "faded" towards their own, the father dying suddenly and the mother more slowly and painfully. "'He would have hated this,'" she observed about her own decline, but "didn't say anything about hating it herself" (393). The mother's impending death introduces another crucial retrospective scene in the novel and a recognition of another ghost, the ghost of Elaine past. Visiting her dying mother, Elaine becomes a version of herself as a child, helping in the garden and with the dishes, doing the laundry, baking muffins. This last activity is especially redolent of the past. The mother, while the two of them were baking muffins, once tried to tell her daughter how to save herself from the suffering inflicted by Cordelia. She is no more successful this time when, again making muffins, she tries to talk to Elaine about the pain she experienced as a child at the hands of "'[t]hose girls.'" "'What girls?'" Elaine responds, even though her fingers "are a wreck" as she "shred[s] them quietly, out of sight beneath the tabletop," something she does "in time of stress" but here chooses to see as only "an old bad habit [she] cannot seem to break" (394).

The mother then suggests that they "sort through the things in the cellar" so that Elaine won't have to do it "'later'" (395) — later, of course, meaning after the mother's death. The sorting venture as a foray into the mother's past is also necessarily a foray into the daughter's as well and a further demonstration of just how much Elaine has mentally consigned to the cellar of her subconscious. Mixed in with such items as wedding pictures, baby clothes (including the single baby sock the mother had knitted before her spontaneous abortion), old bridge tallies, tarnished silverware, and the father's old shoes and boots are Elaine's and Stephen's scrapbooks and childhood drawings along with other items saved from the past of each child. Elaine begins to "catch some of [her mother's] excitement" as she encounters her scrapbook of cut-out women and her old photo album (397). Then she uncovers the most significant item of all. It is her red plastic purse that she can remember taking to church. She remembers the church too: "the onion on the spire, the pews, the stained-glass windows. THE • KINGDOM • OF • GOD • IS • WITHIN • YOU" (397). Something is also within the split, squashed purse. In Elaine's words:

I open it up and take out my blue cat's eye.

"A marble!" says my mother, with a child's delight. "Remember all those marbles Stephen used to collect?"

"Yes," I say. But this one was mine.

I look into it, and see my life entire. (398)

This Proustian moment makes the novel possible. As the previous exchange with her mother about "[t]hose girls" illustrates, Elaine has programmatically forgotten much of her past. This loss of the past is both a version and inversion of death (the loss of the future) and explains why this section of the novel is set against the death of Stephen, for Stephen's actual death parallels Elaine's metaphoric one. Likewise, just as Stephen buries his marbles and then loses the also buried map, Elaine "buries" her one cat's eye marble in her purse, which is then "buried" in the trunk, which is "buried" in the cellar. This Chinese-box series of "burials" also suggests the persistent play at death in the novel, the pretend executions and burials that mirror Elaine's later attempts to bury much of her past. But as both the marble in the purse as well as the first memory prompted by the purse — particularly the message in the stained-glass window, itself an analogue to the marble — imply, what is within can be recovered. The novel itself registers just such a recovery.[3]

To see, however, is not the same as to tell, just as to tell is not the same as to come to terms with, although each item in the sequence is an essential antecedent for the next. This series, starting with the cat's eye marble that gives the work its title, provides the novel's deep structure, which is doubly retrospective and thus reflects, even on the level of design, Atwood's persistent interest in mirror play. More specifically, the retrospective art show and the concomitant retrospective narration of the novel are both a repetition of an earlier looking back, the moment with the marble and the sudden illumination, the resurrection even of Elaine's previously buried past. But the retrospective telling (in the present time) requires a still fuller seeing, and thus Elaine insists on recognizing behind the nineties Toronto to which she returns the old Toronto in which she grew up and persists in revisiting significant sites/sights: the ravine, the lawn where Cordelia threw herself down to make a snow angel, Josef's apartment, the Park Plaza rooftop bar that was formerly a restaurant. She is an artist, and "visuals" are important. Nevertheless, she must finally work into narrative what she formerly worked into her paintings but could not work into words, and so maintained that a painted toaster or wringer, for example, were merely icons of mid-century domesticity and not images of her pain as a child, a pain partly premised on standards of mid-century domesticity. Indeed, when in the narrative present she talks about what is depicted in the paintings, she does the very thing the paintings originally partly precluded and puts into words what they first consigned to silence.

Elaine's story, of course, has been implicit in her paintings all along. Other signs of her painful past also continue to be obvious in the present — for example, the fingers she still gnaws even though she hides them under the table. But to tell her story, she must first come to terms with it, for any narration is a selection and arrangement, a deciding of what details count and to what end; it is never, as Atwood has often insisted, a simple account of the "true story." Thus Elaine, like Offred in *The Handmaid's Tale*, struggles with various versions of her story — the past she claims she has completely forgotten ("'What girls?'"); the past she cannot escape and in which she is permanently trapped ("Get me out of this Cordelia. . . . I don't want to be nine years old forever" [400]). She tries to cast that past into narratable form and also to recast it even as she recounts it. Thus, her last encounter with Jon throws a different retrospective light on her account of their earlier life together — an account framed, as noted, by their final interaction. Elaine's telling of her relationship with Jon thereby becomes one of her triumphs, rather than one of her defeats. She finally confronts their past failure and, at the same time, turns it into something more than that failure.

Much the same point is made in somewhat different form by the titles of the novel's two concluding sections, "Unified Field Theory" and "Bridge," which are themselves versions of each other in that unified field theory is the attempt to connect mathematically — that is, to bridge together — the different basic forces in physics. How do you interconnect the various forces in your life, the different times, places, events, and people who have all influenced you? A partial answer is provided in the penultimate section of the novel as Elaine links the opening of the retrospective show that has brought her back to Toronto with the past out of which the paintings in that show come. More specifically, she sees in the current show an echo of both her first art exhibition and the birthday parties she hated as a child; she also sees versions of her former self in other people at the show, as well as aspects of her paintings that she had not previously discerned. Significantly, she first decides that she has been somewhat foolish in her concern over what she should wear to the opening, a concern expressed throughout the novel and indicative of her desire for socially acceptable disguise (nothing in the guise of something). The black dress she finally buys "looks much the same as all the other black dresses [she has] ever owned" (403). Wearing it, she will look "[n]ice, and negligible" (which isn't the same as nothing); she will, in her own words, "come as I am" (403).

From the vantage point of this present "I am," she soon sees herself as she once was. The bartender, "a severe-eyed young woman" dressed in black, but a more *au-courant* black, serves Elaine with calculated nonchalance and disapproval: "Possibly she wants to be a painter, and thinks I have compromised my principles, knuckled under to success. How I used to revel in such bitter little snobberies myself," Elaine remembers, "how easy they were, once" (403–04). The show is a personal and private retrospective in other ways too. Elaine juxtaposes the "professional-looking computer-and-laser-printer" catalogue Charna has produced with her own memory of the "smeared and illegible" mimeo catalogue of her first show. She also contrasts Charna's feminist commentary on the paintings with her own sense of what they portray and signify. Elaine also finds that her sense of herself is changing, that she notices things she hadn't recognized before. For example, she can "now see" the "considerable malice" as well as the substantial labour that went into the depicting of Mrs. Smeath, whose pallid and ugly body "is there as it was, as plain as bread" (404). But the eyes, she recognizes, show something more. Although still "self-righteous . . . , piggy and smug. . . . they are also defeated eyes, uncertain and melancholy, heavy with un-loved duty. The eyes of someone for whom God was a sadistic old man; the eyes of a small-town threadbare decency." Like the young bartender, this is another version of Elaine: "Mrs. Smeath was a transplant to the city, from somewhere a lot smaller. A displaced person; as [Elaine herself] was." Moreover, she did take Elaine in. "An eye for an eye leads only to more blindness" (405), Elaine concludes, reversing the implications of the title of one of her paintings of Mrs. Smeath — *An Eye for an Eye* — which showed a half-naked potato-faced Mrs. Smeath holding a potato and a potato peeler.

Other "displaced persons" show up in the other paintings: her parents camping in the woods during the war; her brother Stephen as a World War II RCAF officer falling calmly but without a parachute through the sky and holding in his hand a toy wooden sword; her *Three Muses*, Mrs. Finestein, Miss Stuart, and Mr. Banerji, who despite the burden of their own displacement showed Elaine a kindness she could not show to Mrs. Smeath. Elaine herself is also somewhat displaced. In her one self-portrait, entitled *Cat's Eye*, she positions herself, metafictionally and as in the novel itself, partly in the present and partly in the past. The painting shows part of her face, portrayed as aging, with "incipient wrinkles" and a "few grey hairs" (grey hairs that "in reality [she pulls] out"), but a pier-glass reflects the back of the head of a much younger version of herself, as well as three young girls "dressed in the winter clothing of the girls of forty years ago" (408). Elaine also feels displaced in Toronto; even at the show she still thinks she "shouldn't have come back here, to this city that has it in for [her]" (410). Cordelia, too, remains displaced. She doesn't come to the opening, and with that absence something of Elaine is again lost, displaced:

> Really it's Cordelia I expect, Cordelia I want to see. There are things I need to ask her. Not what happened, back then in the time I lost, because now I know that. I need to ask her why. . . .
>
> She will have her own version. I am not the centre of her story, because she herself is that. But I could give her something you can never have, except from another person: what you look like from outside. A reflection. This is the part of herself I could give back to her.
>
> We are like the twins in old fables, each of whom has been given half a key. (411)

All of this reflecting is itself reflected in the last painting in the show, the one Elaine has done most recently, *Unified Field Theory*. In it she portrays a snow-covered wooden bridge, the Virgin of Lost Things floating just above the bridge and holding a blue cat's eye marble where her heart should be. Below the bridge the night sky appears, with "[s]tar upon star" and "swirling nebulae" and "galaxy upon galaxy," like "the universe, in its incandescence and darkness," as "seen through a telescope" (408). That cosmic sky verges into the "stones" and "beetles and small roots" also seen beneath the bridge along with a stream of clear blue water flowing from "underneath the earth," from "the cemetery," from "[t]he land of the dead people." This painting is a summation of Elaine's life as a woman and an artist. It is a prediction, too, of how life and art will be lost in time, as Elaine's reaction upon surveying her paintings suggests:

> I walk the room, surrounded by the time I've made; which is not a place, which is only a blur, the moving edge we live in; which is fluid, which turns back upon itself, like a wave. I may have thought I was preserving something from time, salvaging something; like all those painters, centuries ago, who thought they were bringing Heaven to earth, the revelations of God, the eternal stars, only to have their slabs of wood and plaster stolen, mislaid, burnt, hacked to pieces, destroyed by rot and mildew. (409)

For the moment, however, the paintings are still there and so is she and that is almost enough.

She doesn't encounter Cordelia but, instead, an even more obvious version of her former self. The section of the novel entitled "Unified Field Theory" is itself unified when Elaine recognizes at the end, as she did at the beginning with the bartender, another young woman as a version of her younger self. She also hears that second version consign her paintings to the fate she herself has just predicted:

> [This young woman is] a painter, it goes without saying, but she says it anyway. She's in a mini-skirt and tight leggings and flat clumpy black shoes with laces, her hair is shaved up the back the way my brother's used to be, a late forties square-boy's cut. She is post everything, she is what will come after *post*. She is what will come after me.
>
> "I loved your early work," she says. "*Falling Women*, I loved that. I mean, it sort of summed up an era, didn't it?" She doesn't mean to be cruel, she doesn't know she's just relegated me to the dust-heap along with crank telephones and whalebone stays. (412)

Elaine knows that she would once have "said something annihilating [back] to her," but "what purpose would it serve?" The "past-tense admiration is sincere," and so she "lie[s] through [her] teeth" that she is " 'glad' " to be so praised, silently counting herself lucky to "still have teeth to lie through" (412).

The bartender and the young painter, as versions of Elaine, are also versions of Susie and Cordelia, who as young artists (a painter, an actress) are also versions of Elaine. The young painter is also a double version of Cordelia, the Cordelia Elaine knew as a nine year old and the Cordelia who would now be in her fifties whom Elaine hoped to encounter at the show. She is the first Cordelia with the negative thrust of her praise and her implication that Elaine is becoming "nothing." At the same time, she also provides the "reflection" that Elaine wanted to exchange with Cordelia — the sense of what one looks like to an other. But the implicit criticism in the young artist's praise is not "given back," as the earlier explicit criticism from Cordelia was. The "field" may be the same, but it is negotiated differently. As Elaine observes at the conclusion of this section — and in conjunction with Cordelia who still has a *"tendency to exist,"* who is *"dead"* but won't *"lie down"*: "Never pray for justice, because you might get some" (414).

* * *

In the final section of the novel, "Bridge," Elaine, as earlier noted, revisits the bridge over the ravine and has her concluding encounter with a Cordelia who both is and isn't there. But there is a second bridge in this section as well, the bridge of flight, the airplane. Elaine misses her scheduled flight because she drank too much at the reception, even though she "should know better" — an echo of Cordelia's condemnations in the past but also a suggestion of how minor those charges were (417). On a later flight, she encounters another version of herself and Cordelia, two old women who are what she and Cordelia might have been in the future, just as the two young women in the preceding section suggest what they were in the past. The two are drinking and playing cards, laughing and cheating, making jokes about their frequent trips to the bathroom at the back of the plane:

They have saved up for this trip and they are damn well going to enjoy it, despite the arthritis of one, the swollen legs of the other. They're rambunctious, they're full of beans; they're tough as thirteen, they're innocent and dirty, they don't give a hoot. Responsibilities have fallen away from them, obligations, old hates and grievances; now for a short while they can play again like children, but this time without the pain. (420)

In the shyness and innocence of her last night with Jon, Elaine did experience something of that second chance to replay the past "without the pain." She wishes she could do so in an even more painful context and redeem another and more important relationship: "This is what I miss, Cordelia: not something that's gone, but something that will never happen. Two old women giggling over their tea" (421). Yet there are two old women giggling over their tea who are partly Elaine and Cordelia. They are playing at being children again (with their game of Snap), at being young women again (with their "desiccated mouth[s] lipsticked bright red with bravado" [420]), so they also partly reverse Elaine and Cordelia, who, as children and adolescents, played at being old. Finally, and most importantly, Elaine, for the first time in the novel, now sees in these older woman an image of what she wishes she might become, not of what she desperately does not want to be. A coming to terms with her past is also a coming to terms with her future, and with the fact that she is female. She can at last move beyond her dubious misogyny.

Cat's Eye concludes with Elaine's vision of the night world and her night journey as a reflection of the light and darkness in which she now finds herself.

Now it's full night, clear, moonless and filled with stars, which are not eternal as was once thought, which are not where we think they are. If they were sounds, they would be echoes, of something that happened millions of years ago: a word made of numbers. Echoes of light, shining out of the midst of nothing.

It's old light, and there's not much of it. But it's enough to see by. (421)

Stars, like people, are also displaced. But shining from where they no longer are, they still give enough light to see by. Elaine has emerged from the hell of her past to see it in a different light. As earlier observed, one of the "echoes" in this passage is its evocation of Dante emerging from hell to see the stars as a sign of God's ordering of the heavens and of the full fixed scope and scale of creation. Even if that celestial order no longer holds, the questions it ostensibly answered still pertain: How does one live in the light of what one knows — the disorder of any personal life, the injustice of society (particularly a patriarchal society as it impinges on women and a consumer society as it depletes everything), the chaos of a world intermittently at war, the larger chaos of the universe? Elaine doesn't conclusively answer any of these questions (final answers are in the same unlikely realm as fixed stars), but she comes to see how she has provisionally answered them and to see better the gains and losses of her different answers. It is a recognition towards which we can all aspire.

NOTES

¹ Nathalie Cooke, in "Reading Reflections: The Autobiographical Illusion in *Cat's Eye*," has similarly termed the novel a "fictive autobiography" (164), but she emphasizes that the novel makes use of autobiography — rather than providing it — and so cannot be read as an only slightly disguised account of the author's life. Douglas Glover, in "Her Life Entire," also notes how "Atwood loves to play hide and seek at the place where autobiography and fiction meet" (11).

² Atwood's feminist rewriting of three canonical male writers is obviously similar to Alice Munro's earlier deployment of Homer, Milton, and Keats in *Who Do You Think You Are?* In each case the woman author avoids a Bloomian and masculinist *Anxiety of Influence* Oedipal conflict.

³ A parallel recovery is also registered in the novel. As McCombs observes, the five paintings that Elaine does after finding her marble all "look backwards or inwards in time, to re-member and re-create those lost and buried: her dead parents; her three muses, each aliens bearing alien gifts; her dead brother; the *Cat's Eye* self-portrait; and the Virgin of Lost Things" (13).

Works Cited

Ahern, Stephen. " 'Meat Like You Like It': The Production of Identity in Atwood's 'Cat's Eye.' " *Canadian Literature* 137 (1993): 8–17.

Advances the rather contradictory claims that "*Cat's Eye* is a case study in the pathology of female identity construction" in patriarchal society (8) and that "the forces that distort and weaken Elaine's confidence and place her in a contradictory subject-position are overwhelmingly female" (13).

Atwood, Margaret. *Bodily Harm*. Toronto: McClelland, 1981.

——. *Cat's Eye*. Toronto: McClelland, 1988.

——. *The Circle Game*. Toronto: Anansi, 1967.

——. *The Edible Woman*. Toronto: McClelland, 1969.

——. *The Handmaid's Tale*. Toronto: McClelland, 1985.

——. *Interlunar*. Toronto: Oxford UP, 1984.

——. *Lady Oracle*. Toronto: McClelland, 1976.

——. *Life Before Man*. Toronto: McClelland, 1979.

——. *Power Politics*. Toronto: Anansi, 1971.

——. *The Robber Bride*. Toronto: McClelland, 1993.

——. *Selected Poems II: Poems Selected and New; 1976–1986*. Boston: Houghton Mifflin, 1987.

——. *Surfacing*. Toronto: McClelland, 1972.

——. *Survival: A Thematic Guide to Canadian Literature*. Toronto: Anansi, 1972.

——. *True Stories*. Toronto: Oxford UP, 1981.

——. *Wilderness Tips*. Toronto: McClelland, 1991.

Banerjee, Chinmoy. "Atwood's Time: Hiding Art in *Cat's Eye*." *Modern Fiction Studies* 36 (1990): 513–22.

Emphasizes how the novel turns, narratively and psychologically, on Elaine's hiding a painful relationship with her family as well as with Cordelia.

Bautch, Richard. "*Cat's Eye* by Margaret Atwood." *America* 6 May 1989: 435–37.

A summary review that focuses on Elaine and ignores Cordelia.

Beran, Carol. "Images of Women's Power in Contemporary Canadian Fiction by Women." *Studies in Canadian Literature* 15.2 (1990): 55–76.

Compares how Margaret Atwood, Alice Munro, and Aritha van Herk portray women's victimization and their transcendence of this victim status.

Bettelheim, Bruno. *The Uses of Enchantment: The Meaning and Importance of Fairy Tales*. New York: Knopf, 1976.

Bloom, Harold. *The Anxiety of Influence*. New York: Oxford UP, 1973.

Bottigheimer, Ruth B. *Grimms' Bad Girls and Bad Boys: The Moral and Social Vision of the Tales*. New Haven: Yale UP, 1987.

Bouson, J. Brooks. *Brutal Choreographies: Oppositional Strategies and Narrative Design in the Novels of Margaret Atwood*. Amherst: U of Massachusetts P, 1993. 159–84.

The chapter entitled "The Power Politics of Women's Relationships in *Cat's Eye*" provides a feminist reading of the construction of femininity and shows how the novel enacts the transformation of pain into art.

Brookner, Anita. "Unable to Climb Out of the Abyss." *Spectator* 28 Jan. 1989: 32–33.

A positive review that praises the novel's portrayal of the traumas of childhood.

Cixous, Hélène. "The Laugh of the Medusa." *Signs* 1 (1976): 875–93.

Cleavor, Carole. "Life Without Joy." *New Leader* 6 Mar. 1989: 19.

Finds Elaine to be too negative a protagonist and the novel to be "a cold book . . . devoid of feeling" (19).

Cooke, Nathalie. "The Politics of Ventriloquism: Margaret Atwood's Fictive Confessions." *Various Atwoods: Essays on the Later Poems, Short Fiction, and Novels*. Ed. Lorraine M. York. Concord, ON: Anansi, 1995. 207–28.

A study of Atwood's use of the confessional form to achieve rhetorical and ethical objectives.

——. "Reading Reflections: The Autobiographical Illusion in *Cat's Eye*." *Essays on Life Writing: From Genre to Critical Practice*. Ed. Marlene Kadar. Toronto: U of Toronto P, 1992. 162–70.

Assesses how Atwood uses autobiographical elements in the novel to challenge the reader, forestall closure, and resist classification.

Cowart, David. "Bridge and Mirror: Replicating Selves in *Cat's Eye*." *Postmodern Fiction in Canada*. Ed. Theo D'haen and Hans Bertens. Amsterdam: Rodopi, 1992. 125–36.

Assesses *Cat's Eye*, with reference to many literary analogues, as a novel of a divided self, but sees Elaine to be finally reintegrated through her commitment to art and honest representation.

Crosbie, Lynn. "Like a Hook into a *Cat's Eye*: Locating Margaret Atwood's Susie." *Tessera* 15 (1993): 30–41.

Criticizes Atwood for failing to recognize the parallels between Susie and Elaine but fails to recognize that it is Atwood who worked these similarities into the novel in the first place.

Dante (Alighieri). *The Inferno*. Trans. John Ciardi. New York: NAL, 1954.

Davey, Frank. *Post-National Arguments: The Politics of the Anglophone-Canadian Novel since 1967*. Toronto: U of Toronto P, 1993. 223–39.

One chapter entitled "Individualist Nationalism: *Cat's Eye*" argues that the novel is an attempt to validate a dubious individualism in a "pure northern Canada, in which social codes of all kinds are intrusions on identity" (239).

Duffy Dennis. Rev. of *Cat's Eye*. *University of Toronto Quarterly* 59 (1989): 13–14.

Maintains that Elaine is unconvincing as a protagonist, a painter, and a victim.

Dundes, Alan, ed. *Little Red Riding Hood: A Casebook*. Madison: U of Wisconsin P, 1989.

French, William. "A Dangerous Meadow." *Globe and Mail* [Toronto] 1 Oct. 1988: C21.

A brief review that considers the novel antifeminist.

Gernes, Sonia. "Transcendent Women: Uses of the Mystical in Margaret Atwood's *Cat's Eye* and Marilynne Robinson's *Housekeeping*." *Religion and Literature* 23.3 (1991): 143–65.

Argues that in both novels the mystical functions to counter the patriarchal; sees mysticism, science, and feminism as constituting the "unified field" of *Cat's Eye*.

Givner, Jessie. "Names, Faces and Signatures in Margaret Atwood's 'Cat's Eye' and 'The Handmaid's Tale.'" *Canadian Literature* 133 (1992): 56–75.

Argues that *Cat's Eye* undermines such dichotomies as autobiography/fiction, figuration/disfiguration, and naming/misnaming. Also notes parallels with Lucy Maud Montgomery's *Anne of Green Gables* and Alfred Tennyson's "Lancelot and Elaine."

Glover, Douglas. "Her Life Entire." *Books in Canada* Oct. 1988: 11–14.

This very perceptive overview assesses the skill, craft, and playfulness with which the novel is put together.

Golding, William. *Lord of the Flies*. 1955. New York: Capricorn, 1959.

Grace, Sherrill. "Gender as Genre: Atwood's Autobiographical 'I.'" *Margaret Atwood: Writing and Subjectivity*. Ed. Colin Nicholson. New York: St. Martin's, 1994. 189–204.

Assesses the connections between fictive biography and gender in *Lady Oracle*, *The Handmaid's Tale*, and *Cat's Eye*.

——. "Theory and Practice." *Canadian Literature* 127 (1990): 135–38.

A comparative review of *Cat's Eye* and *The Private Self: Theory and Practice of Women's Autobiographical Writing* (edited by Shari Benstock) that praises *Cat's Eye* for its depth and vision.

Greene, Gayle. *Changing the Story: Feminist Fiction and the Tradition*. Bloomington: Indiana UP, 1991. 207–14.

This critique of *Cat's Eye* as a deeply misogynistic novel was originally published as a book review in *Women's Studies* 18 (1991): 445–55.

Hengen, Shannon. *Margaret Atwood's Power: Mirrors, Reflections and Images in Select Fiction and Poetry*. Toronto: Second Story, 1993.

Cat's Eye is briefly assessed in terms of Atwood's feminism, nationalism, and tricks with mirrors.

Hite, Molly. "An Eye for an I: The Disciplinary Society in *Cat's Eye.*" *Various Atwoods: Essays on the Later Poems, Short Fiction, and Novels.* Ed. Lorraine M. York. Concord, ON: Anansi, 1995. 191–206.

A Foucauldian reading of how Elaine is constructed as a necessarily imperfect female subject but finally comes to a feminist realization of the imperfections of the patriarchal disciplinary society that so constructed her.

Howells, Coral Ann. *Margaret Atwood.* Macmillan Modern Novelists. Houndmills: Macmillan, 1996. 148–60.

The chapter entitled "Atwood's Retrospective Art: *Cat's Eye*" uses Paul de Man's "Autobiography as De-facement" to assess the double figuration of Elaine in her paintings and narrative. An earlier version of this chapter, "*Cat's Eye*: Elaine Risley's Retrospective Art," appeared in *Margaret Atwood: Writing and Subjectivity.* Ed. Colin Nicholson. New York: St. Martin's, 1994. 204–18.

Ingersoll, Earl G., ed. *Margaret Atwood: Conversations.* Princeton: Ontario Review, 1990.

A collection of major interviews. Only the last one, "Waltzing Again" (conducted by Earl G. Ingersoll), deals with *Cat's Eye* (234–38).

—. "Margaret Atwood's 'Cat's Eye': Re-Viewing Women in a Postmodern World." ARIEL: *A Review of International English Literature* 22.4 (1991): 17–27.

An overview that discusses Atwood's use of her own past and her treatment of mothering in the novel.

Kanfer, Stefan. "Time Arrested." *Time* 6 Feb. 1989: 70.

A review that praises the novel's treatment of childhood.

Koenig, Rhoda. "Hell to Pay." *New York* 13 Feb. 1989: 80–81.

A very negative review.

Lane, R.D. "Cordelia's 'Nothing': The Character of Cordelia and Margaret Atwood's *Cat's Eye.*" *Essays on Canadian Writing* 48 (1992–93): 73–88.

Sees the novel as a contemporary feminist reworking of Shakespeare's *King Lear.*

LeBihan, Jill. "*The Handmaid's Tale, Cat's Eye* and *Interlunar*: Margaret Atwood's Feminist(?) Futures(?)." *Narrative Strategies in Canadian Literature: Feminism and Postcolonialism.* Ed. Coral Ann Howells, et al. Milton Keynes: Open UP, 1991. 93–107.

Mainly about *The Handmaid's Tale.*

LeClaire, Jacques. "Margaret Atwood's *Cat's Eye* as a Portrait of the Artist." *Commonwealth* 13 (1990): 73–80.

A summary of the novel that focuses on its possible autobiographical basis and its concern with artistic creation.

Lee, Hermione. "Little Women." *New Republic* 10 Apr. 1989: 38–40.

A review that suggests Atwood is disengaging from feminism in this novel.

Lurie, Alison. "The Mean Years." *Ms.* Mar. 1989: 38–39.

A very positive summary review.

Mackay, Shena. "The Painter's Revenges." *Times Literary Supplement* 3–9 Feb. 1989: 113.

A brief review that praises *Cat's Eye* for its description of childhood pains and perceptions and judges it "Atwood's best novel to date."

Manguel, Alberto. "First Impressions." *Saturday Night* Nov. 1988: 66–69.

Considers the novel an archetypal treatment of the pain of childhood.

McCombs, Judith. "Contrary Re-memberings: The Creating Self and Feminism in *Cat's Eye.*"*Canadian Literature* 129 (1991): 9–23.

A feminist reading that is particularly persuasive on the significance of Elaine's paintings.

McDermott, Alice. "What Little Girls Are Really Made Of." *New York Times Book Review* 5 Feb. 1989: 1, 35.

A summary review that finds the novel to be "Atwood's most emotionally engaging fiction thus far" (35).

Munro, Alice. *Who Do You Think You Are?* Toronto: Macmillan, 1978.

Osborne, Carol. "Constructing the Self Through Memory: *Cat's Eye* as a Novel of Female Development." *Frontiers* 14.3 (1994): 95–112.

Argues that "[i]n her concern with memory [and] with the need for her protagonist to confront the past in coming to know herself, Atwood most resembles contemporary African-American novelists" (100).

Proust, Marcel. *Remembrance of Things Past.* Trans. C.K. Scott Moncrieff. 2 vols. New York: Random House, 1934.

Rao, Eleanor. *Strategies for Identity: The Fiction of Margaret Atwood.* Writing about Women: Feminist Literary Studies. New York: Lang, 1993.

Assesses Atwood's fiction in terms of how it represents the female subject as a provisional and shifting construct.

Robinson, Lillian S. "Coming of Age in Toronto." *Nation* 5 June 1989: 776–79.

Argues that *Cat's Eye* fails because Elaine's vision is too limited and self-centred.

Rooke, Constance. Rev. of *Cat's Eye. Malahat Review* 85 (1988): 131–32.

Judges *Cat's Eye* to be a "brilliant new novel" that is "more personal" and "more metafictional" than its predecessors (131).

Shakespeare, William. *King Lear.* Ed. Barbara A. Mowat and Paul Werstine. The New Folger Library Shakespeare. New York: Washington Square, 1993.

——. *Macbeth.* Ed. Barbara A. Mowat and Paul Werstine. The New Folger Library Shakespeare. New York: Washington Square, 1992.

Sharpe, Martha. "Margaret Atwood and Julia Kristeva: Space-Time, the Dissident Woman Artist, and the Pursuit of Female Solidarity in *Cat's Eye.*" *Essays on Canadian Writing* 50 (1993): 174–89.

Stresses the feminist implications of Elaine's paintings and how they point the way to a space-time different from male linearity in space and time.

Staels, Hilde. *Margaret Atwood's Novels: A Study of Narrative Discourse.* Tübingen: Verlag, 1995. 177–91.

One chapter entitled "*Cat's Eye*: Creating a Symbolic Space Out of Lost Time" stresses the importance of ironic mirroring in the novel and the ways in which both Cordelia and Mrs. Smeath are doubles of Elaine.

Strehle, Susan. *Fiction and the Quantum Universe*. Chapel Hill: U of North Carolina P, 1992.

One chapter entitled "Margaret Atwood: *Cat's Eye* and the Subjective Author" sees the novel as a critique of the high cost — both social and individual — of casting women as objects and as an account of Elaine's refusal to be so cast.

Thompson, Sharon. "Sugar and Spite: Margaret Atwood's Growing Pains." *Village Voice* 21 Mar. 1989: 49–50.

Considers the novel "a critique of gender segregation" but one that "doesn't reveal much about what goes wrong between most women" (50).

Thurman, Judith. "When You Wish Upon a Star." *New Yorker* 29 May 1989: 108–10.

Judges *Cat's Eye* to be beautifully written but suggests that it, like *The Handmaid's Tale*, fails to find its real subject, which, this reviewer suggests, is a woman's complicity in her victimization.

Timson, Judith. "Atwood's Triumph." *Maclean's* 3 Oct. 1988: 56–61.

More a review of Atwood's previous writing career and her rise to international prominence than of *Cat's Eye*.

Towers, Robert. "Mystery Women." *New York Review of Books* 27 Apr. 1989: 50–52.

Sees *Cat's Eye* as too autobiographical but praises its comprehensiveness as a social history of mid-century North America.

Wilson, Sharon Rose. *Margaret Atwood's Fairy-Tale Sexual Politics*. Jackson: UP of Mississippi, 1993. 295–314.

The chapter entitled "*Cat's Eye* Vision: 'Rapunzel' and 'The Snow Queen' " sets forth a reading of the novel in terms of two fairy-tale intertexts to show how Elaine frees herself from the captivity of Toronto and her past and from the limitations of a cold marble vision. An earlier version of this chapter, "Margaret Atwood: Eyes and I's," appeared in *International Literature in English: Essays on the Major Writers*. Ed. Robert L. Ross. New York: Garland, 1991. 225–39.

Woolf, Virginia. *To the Lighthouse*. New York: Harcourt, 1927.

York, Lorraine M. " 'Over All I Place a Glass Bell': The Meta-Iconography of Margaret Atwood." *Various Atwood's: Essays on the Later Poems, Short Fiction, and Novels* Ed. Lorraine M. York. Concord, ON: Anansi, 1995. 229–52.

Examines Atwood's use of icons, including her own status as a literary icon.

Zipes, Jack. *The Trials and Tribulations of Little Red Riding Hood*. South Hadley, MA: Bergin and Garvey, 1983.

Index

**AGMV
MARQUIS**
Québec, Canada
1997